D0475730

The Sacrifice

The Sacrifice

Mike Uden

ROBERT HALE · LONDON

ISBN 978-0-7198-0822-7

Robert Hale Limited
Clerkenwell House
Clerkenwell Green
London EC1R 0HT

www.halebooks.com

2 4 6 8 10 9 7 5 3

Thanks to Jan for all her patience and to the children and
grandchildren for just being great. Also thanks to PCP.

Typeset in 11 / 15pt Palatino
Printed in the UK by Berforts Information Press Ltd

ONE

'WELL, YES, OF course I've heard of her.'

And so started my involvement in the very strange case of Su A; or, perhaps, the very strange case of the *disappearing* Su A. This was a missing person case that, having immediately hit the local press, had briefly gone national, featuring in a documentary where a furrowed-brow investigative journalist had suggested, controversially, that the British police put greater resources behind missing Brits – particularly white, middle-class, attractive ones – than missing blacks, Asians and foreigners. After that she'd slipped slowly out of the nation's consciousness, turning up briefly on another crime-time special about young runaways and then a couple more times in the local press. Since then, nothing.

And there I sat, some three months later, in my little office-above-the-shops, with an impassively faced Korean in front of me, asking if I'd heard of her. So yes, of course I'd heard of her. What I hadn't said, of course, was that she was probably dead by now. Most girls who go missing for that length of time turn up – assuming they ever do turn up – as a decomposing corpse in a shallow grave.

Su A Kim (the 'A' was not an initial, but part of her name – and pronounced softly, as in 'cat') was a twenty-four-year-old South Korean student attending an English-language school in South London. On a wet Saturday in September she and five of her friends had taken the bus from Kent House to Bromley, before spending the afternoon traipsing around The Glades shopping centre (CCTV footage available), walking to the Market Square, sitting in Costa sipping coffees, then walking back to the bus stop (more CCTV) and taking the bus back home. Except Su A, that is. She'd said goodbye, then walked around the corner towards another bus stop, for the 162. This bus takes a far less direct route, but does drop off nearer her landlady's doorstep, and it was tipping down at the time. Unfortunately, although the 162 should have had CCTV, this one didn't. All we do know is that she never arrived home.

No one had been charged; no one had even been detained. Precious little in the way of evidence too, forensic or otherwise – just the disappearance. Could she have absconded? Unlikely. She was a foreign student with very little English and no local connections. In fact, apart from her landlady and a few fellow students – all also foreign – she knew no one. Girls like that just didn't disappear. Unless …

There was just one, very tenuous lead. After she had left her student friends, one of them – a fellow Korean called Chen Choi – had allegedly received a frantic phone call from her. The single Korean word, mudang. This, apparently, means fortune teller. And this may well have been the main reason it was news-worthy in the first place –'Missing Su in Fortune Teller Mystery' being a headline writer's dream.

You may notice that I said Chen Choi allegedly received this mudang call. This is because he then left his mobile on the bus. Brilliant.

'But, er, Mr Hye …'

'Hyeon-gi,' he prompted, before spelling it out letter by letter, then suggesting I just call him Ko.

'Yes, well, Ko, why would you want me to look into some-thing the police are still in the middle of?'

'In the middle of?' he laughed. 'Sixteen weeks is hardly "in the middle of", is it?'

'Well, these things do take time.'

'You sound like the police.'

'Maybe that's because I was once. And once a copper … Seriously, though, they may be closer than you think – often are.'

'And often aren't too. In this case, anyway.'

'What makes you say that?'

'Because I represent her family and if anyone knows, they do.'

I thought for a while: 'OK, but I'm honestly not sure getting me involved would be helpful. Or appropriate.'

'Appropriate?'

'Well, while the case is still open, I mean. While the police are still working on it.'

A slight flicker of irritation, a tiny stiffening of his jaw, told me that my taking the police's line on this didn't exactly please him. 'What you mean, Ms Andrews, is that your police are sooo wonderful –' He was slightly hamming an American accent for the *sooo wonderful* '– that we foreigners should just trust you all implicitly.'

'Well, that's not exactly what I meant, no …'

'You know, when a young English girl goes missing abroad –' He then looked at me, paused, and added '– *in Portugal, say*. There doesn't seem to be such reticence, does there? Your investigators are on a plane within the week.'

'OK, fair point,' I said. 'But why me?'

'Why not?' he asked, shrugging. 'You're local, you're a private investigator, and as you said – you're ex police.'

Again, fair point. But there was still something that didn't quite ring true about this guy. Perhaps he was just a little too smug. Or it could even have been what he was wearing. You may laugh, but character-wise, these things count. You see, I sort of mistrust collarless tops. Don't know why, but it's clearly not just me. Cat-stroking Bond villains, Nazi storm troopers, bogus mystics, dodgy clerics – not a collar between them. And this Mr Ko Hyeon-gi, under his expensive jacket, was wearing a collarless shirt, with mother-of-pearl buttons – done right up to his neck.

He left my office as civilly, if perhaps slightly creepily, as he'd entered – giving me a damp handshake at my office door.

I went back to my desk, sat down and thought. Should I or shouldn't I? He'd made it pretty clear that if I didn't, someone else would. In fact, even if I said yes, he might still take his trade elsewhere. He was the buyer, I was the merchandise – that much was clear.

I needed to weigh up the pros and cons. Firstly, it would be a massive change to my normal line of work. Like other female investigators – of which there aren't too many – my mainstay was partner surveillance. Stock-in-trade for my market. After all, if a woman suspects there's something dodgy going on in her relationship, it's the one time she definitely *won't* be trusting men. I could confide with her too, in a way men simply can't. So part detective, part agony aunt. Anyway, send a thief to catch a thief. I've been there. I'm a divorcee.

I slid my notepad towards me, turned to a blank page, drew a line right down the centre, put a plus sign top left and a minus sign in the top right. I then added the word *'Different'* to the positive column. I thought for a moment. Is doing something different always a positive? No. So I wrote the word *'Different'* in the right-hand column too.

Next consideration: money. What he was offering was crap – totally unrelated to any advertised rates. One whole month of looking into every aspect of a very cold case, with the police obstructing me at every turn. In the real world, there are no Holmes and Watsons. Private investigators don't have cosy chats at crime scenes. Nor do they stoop over bodies in morgues, check forensic evidence through microscopes or leaf through police interview transcripts. In fact, I cannot think of anyone less welcome in a police station than a private detective. Criminals get a better reception! And for this fruitless and frustrating task I would receive the princely sum of one thousand pounds. Thank God for police pensions.

So I wrote *'Money'* in the negative column.

On the other hand, it *was* money – and I had no other work on. So I wrote *'Money'* in the positive column too.

Next: publicity. Did I want it; did I *need* it? Mr Hyeon-gi had made it pretty clear that it was his trump card – why he could offer me, and any another other agent he was chatting up, such a paltry sum. So if I didn't take it, some other private dick (how apt) certainly would. OK, the Su A case was no longer exactly hot news, but it was news. In fact, thinking about it, that could well be part of her family's thinking. Employ an agent, tell the press, and stoke it all up again. But at fifty-four years of age, I certainly didn't need stoking up.

I scribbled *'Publicity'* in the negative column. I leaned back on my chair. Outside, bare winter trees shivered against a winter sky. Would it only be negative? I would probably never, ever get a chance like this again. Even if it only made local TV news – me leaving my front door, files under one arm, a briefcase in the other. Would that be so bad? Anna, for one, would be proud. Her old mum making a few waves.

Then a luscious if rather infantile thought flashed through my mind. David. My ex. The same David who had originally left me because he was 'suffocating' and 'in a rut', who 'wanted a challenge' and 'needed extending'. Funny the way men only seem to become extended and de-suffocated with woman fifteen years their junior, isn't it? Especially – and I must confess to a touch of bitterness here – when the so-called suffo-cater is trying her hardest to keep reasonably fit and young looking – watching her weight, going to the gym and looking vaguely stylish. And especially when the suffocatee has a beer belly and no dress sense. Well, since then, apart from de-suffo-cating himself with his young 'challenge' on a Goan beach for six months, he'd done precisely nothing – back in Blighty, suntan faded, patchouli evaporated, hippy sex-friend gone. Oh yes, and no house – I get the semi, he gets the bedsit. Childish thought, but delicious. His suffocating little in-a-rut wifey turning up on TV.

So I quickly jotted 'Publicity' on the plus side and looked at the paper. Three pros and three cons. All identical.

I needed some air. I put on my coat, locked up my office, and descended, via the rickety stairs, to the street. The sky was turning from a cold grey to an even colder, if clearer, blue. I walked the short distance to the park, taking the path which climbed quickly and steeply, from the built-up little valley in which I live and work, to the windswept open space at the top of the hill. I had done this many times before – even jogged it – but still found it tough.

Huffing and puffing inelegantly – it really is a steep hill – I flopped down on a bench and, looking up, took in the view. Below me was my suburban valley. Rising from that – in semis and terraces – were a thousand people's lives. You only need a small proportion of them – say one per cent – to screw up so badly to keep the likes of me employed permanently. Perhaps I should simply forget this case. Wait for the next relationship wreck.

I raised my eyes further, to the skeletal peak of the Crystal Palace mast. Not exactly spectacular, but strangely uplifting. You could almost imagine an ancient BBC logo spinning around it and a scratchy newsreel soundtrack.

You know, there was one very good reason *not* to take this assignment. It would fail. Definitely. If the police had drawn a blank, given their resources, what earthly chance would I stand? I would end up a failure, if not in the eyes of the public – which didn't bother me – then definitely in the eyes of my old police colleagues – which did. Not only would I fail, I'd fall out with them. And I didn't need that.

So, finally, would I take it? Absolutely not.

TWO

'I'LL TAKE IT … if the offer's still open, that is.'

There was a brief, tinny silence on the end of the line.

'Well, yes …'

'So am I … I mean, are you still considering hiring me?'

'Well, yes … yes.'

'Good,' I replied, not entirely convinced it was good. 'I do have a couple of questions though.'

'OK.'

'Well, I suppose they're not so much questions as, well, conditions – of employment, I mean. You see, I've spent a lifetime working for the police, so I obviously know how they … and I'm not prepared to take this on unless … unless it's with their full knowledge. I won't say their consent or cooperation, because they won't give either. In fact they'll probably be, well … unhelpful. But with their knowledge.'

'OK, makes sense. Frankly, we couldn't keep it secret anyway.'

'Yes, exactly. But what I mean is that I'm not prepared to work *against* them.'

'I wouldn't dream of asking you to, Ms Andrews.'

I told him he could call me Pamela and he reminded me to call him Ko. So all nice and cosy, then.

'The point is I'll only take this on if I'm allowed to disclose everything … to the police, I mean.'

'Of course – I'd like to think you would.'

'And I promise you I won't – *we* won't – get anything back.

Because that's the way it works. I've been there. I can see it from their perspective – but that won't stop me telling them everything I know.'

'OK, I can understand why you'd want to keep in with your old friends.'

'Never mind old friends, I just want to keep within the law.'

'Quite so. No problem. And er ... was there something else?'

'Something else?'

'Yes, you said you had a couple of points.'

'Oh yes. You see, I don't want this to turn into some kind of media circus. If I can do this without it being all over the TV, I'd be far happier.'

(Breathing apart, another long silence.)

'That's going to be a bit of a tough call.'

'I don't see why.'

'Well, simply because ... surely it'll find its way into the papers anyway?'

'Maybe it will, maybe it won't. But there's no need to encourage them, is there?'

Given the silence that followed, yes, apparently there was. I would even go so far as to say that getting the media back on board could be his – and therefore presumably Su A's parents' – prime motive.

And if it was, I suppose I could see their point. First they lose their daughter, now they were losing the public. What had started with sympathy was fading into indifference. And the tragedy is, I can see how and why.

In Britain, as in most places, when a pretty girl goes missing, it tugs at the heartstrings. And in Su A's case, being a *foreign* pretty girl – here to learn English – it made it worse. After all, she trusted us, she *chose* us. We feel additional guilt – like hearing that a tourist's been mugged on the Piccadilly line – but far, far worse. We feel partly responsible. So yes, it's newsworthy.

But slowly, something else takes over. The subtle xenophobia.

The hidden racism. Su A was different. That face looking back at you from your morning newspaper doesn't look like your daughter's face. And slowly, but not *that* slowly, she's pushed to the back of our minds.

So where, in this big picture, did I come in? Well, what Ko Hyeon-gi was confirming, despite his best attempts to the contrary, was a little niggle that had been growing in my mind since before I'd decided, after all, to take the job.

Yes, he'd chosen me because I was cheap and probably he'd chosen me because I was local, but mostly he'd chosen me because I was a woman. A woman that (hopefully) looked half-decent, or at least a bit different. That would put it back on the front pages. After all, women detectives are a bit of a novelty, aren't they? And maybe, just maybe, a woman could help push up the ratings, get a bit more airtime. Ideally they'd have gone for a cross between Cheryl Cole and Jordan, but ex-policewomen tend not to look that way. So beggars can't be choosers. If they can't find foxy-chick detectives, they'd go for glamorous grans.

My guess is that he doesn't, for one minute, expect me to get anywhere on this case. Finding Su A, or her body (let's face it, it's a murder by now) would remain the police's job. I was just eye candy – albeit fifty-four-year-old eye candy, if that isn't a contradiction in terms. That was my take on it. Unless I was being over-suspicious – which I have been known to be. It's in my job description, after all.

I could have, perhaps should have, voiced all this to Hyeon-gi – in a very diplomatic way, of course. But I didn't. And the reason I didn't was not cowardice, not even solicitousness. It was because – as I sat there, phone in hand, listening to him going on about some big press conference he wanted to give, while gazing out over winter treetops – my mobile phone suddenly rang.

Illuminating the screen, as it vibrated on my desk, was the most important name in the world: Anna. My daughter. She *always* came first. So I gave him a half-baked excuse, promised to ring him back, and just about managed to catch her call before it switched to voicemail.

'Hi, love, how are you?'

'I'm, er, OK.'

Now I don't know about you, but when it's someone you love, someone you've known forever, there's OK and there's OK. This was definitely the latter.

'I wonder if I could, er, come round, Mum?'

'Of course. Is there anything wrong?'

'No, no.' (Which sounded like yes, yes.) 'I'll tell you when I get there. Shall I come to your office?'

'No, I'll see you at home, if you like.'

'OK, see you in about half an hour. Bye, Mum.'

Now at this point I need to explain the word 'office' and I need to explain the word 'home'. My 'office', as I mentioned before, was just a rented room – plus toilet – above a pet shop, in a row of suburban shops between beautiful Bromley and glamorous Penge. As for the word 'home', that too was deceiving, because it was no longer really Anna's home – but old habits....

I live in a 1930s semi, at the bottom of the Shortlands Valley, just ten minutes walk from my work. Anna moved out a couple of years ago – to a poky flatshare in New Cross, an area of south London she called edgy and I called ugly (and terrifying, and I-really-don't-want-you-to-live-there-Anna). So in one sense, I was always pleased to get her back 'home' – though not if it meant there was some kind of problem, which I was pretty sure there was.

Forty minutes later, as promised, she arrived. And even without warning I'd still have known it was her. Whether lugging grunge-filled sacks of Glastonbury washing, or weighed down by gap-year backpacks, or pulling the arm of a new boyfriend, I could instantly recognize her – even through the rippled glass of my front door. The most familiar entity in the known universe.

I opened the door, she put her rucksack down and, with her eyes already filling up, said: 'I've been made redundant, Mum.'

I flung my arms around her, hugged her and softly patted her back – as I had done so many times in the past – soothing away everything from baby burps to bastard boyfriends. Oh, the joys of motherhood.

We repaired to the lounge and I did the other thing mums do best – go to the kitchen and make her a nice hot cuppa.

It had been her first real job since leaving uni – one she had stuck with, one she had high hopes for – working as a researcher for a TV production company in Soho (she'd never wanted to join the police and I certainly wasn't encouraging her). Her next step up the ladder could have been producer. Could have been. Now, apparently, it couldn't.

I rejoined her with tea and biscuits, and she told me all about it – how times were tough in independent TV – the recession had affected advertising, which in turn had affected TV stations. Up until then they'd had two researchers. Two had just become one. And that's what made it all the worse. If a whole company closes, so be it. But when only one is chosen, it hurts all the more. More like a sacking than a redundancy. So even though she was bemoaning the loss of material things – the pay, the perks, the Friday nights – it was her self-esteem that had taken the real battering. That's what was in need of repair.

We spent ages talking – time was the one thing I could always give her – with me talking things up: the new contacts; the experience; the better-than-before CV; and that a short break would do her good. Accentuate the positive was all I could do. Eventually, saying little, she traipsed upstairs to her teenage bedroom, sat mournfully in front of her mirror and then, an hour later, came back down looking a little more resilient, a little more up for the fight. She'd even washed her face and applied some new make-up.

I made up my mind not to hug her again or say anything too sympathetic – that would simply take us back to where we started – but got up, drew the curtains, lit the gas fire, found a bottle of red and suggested a takeaway pizza.

I hadn't really given the Su A thing a thought. From the moment I'd got Anna's call, I suppose I'd reverted to mum mode. But then, as I walked back into the room, with two glasses in my hand, the day's events came back. And an idea struck me. An absolute brainwave.

There, curled up on the sofa, managing to look both tired and lovely at the same time, as only youth can, was Hyeon-gi's answer. If they wanted an angle – an angle that would bring the Su A story back to life – there it was. An edge? How about a mother and daughter team? Eye candy? What about a twenty-three-year-old blonde, blue-eyed assistant detective? TV ratings? I'd give them TV ratings.

I sat down in the chair opposite, rather than on the sofa next to her, and thought for a second. I needed to take some time, take things slowly.

'I've had this thought, Anna.'

'What's that?'

'Well …you'll need some time to do some research – for work, I mean – won't you?'

'Yes, once I get my head round it.'

'So you'll need a computer.'

'I've got a BlackBerry, Mum.'

'Would that be the "have-you-seen-my-mobile-anywhere" BlackBerry?' I asked.

'Point taken,' she said.

'Look, surely a nice warm office and a phone and a computer would be better.'

She paused for a second, narrowed her eyes a little and said: 'OK, Mum, what are you cooking up?'

'I'm not *cooking up* anything. I was just wondering if you'd like to help me – on a project, I mean?'

'Well,' she said, 'I'm always happy to help, you know that –' (no comment) '– so what kind of project is it?'

'Oh, you know,' I said, counter-shrugging, 'doing what I normally do … a little bit of detective work. It could keep you occupied for a few weeks – earn you a few bob while you're doing your research.'

Suddenly, all the shrugging was gone – replaced by incredulity. '*Me* help *you* with *detective* work?'

I adjusted my position in the chair, getting the cushion into a more comfortable position and using up a few more strategic seconds.

'Look, Anna,' I said, picking up my glass, 'you probably can't see the logic of this at the moment. If I were in your position, I wouldn't either. But you'll have to bear with me. I promise I'll fill you in later … as to why you'd be perfect, I mean.'

'Why can't you tell me now?'

That's the trouble with children, isn't it? Why, why, why.

I put my glass down and thought. 'Well, if the person who's employing me reacts to my idea in the way I'd expect, I'll know for sure. Then I can tell you.'

'All very mystifying,' she said.

'Goes with the territory.'

'Yes, Mum, but I thought the mysteries normally surrounded the cases, not the detectives.'

'Fair enough. But for now, you'll just have to trust me. I think you can be very useful. And if I'm right, they'll jump at the chance of getting you on board. If I'm wrong, so be it – nothing ventured …'

'Look,' she said, softening her voice a little, 'I don't want charity. I know you, Mum. You'll find a way of putting money into my pocket. It's a lovely thought, but I don't need it. I'll get by. Anyway, they gave me over a month's salary, so I'm OK for now.'

'OK.' I shrugged. 'Let's forget it for now. It's no big deal, but if you're interested I could speak to them; it wouldn't be charity. It certainly wouldn't come from my fee; they'd have to pay extra.'

I sat back into the chair. 'And as for *how* you could help, well, I'd need loads of research because I wouldn't have access to police files – and you're a million times better at that than me. It's what you do!'

'Police files! What's all this about, Mum?'

'It's, er … a missing person job.'

She narrowed her pretty eyes again. *'Missing person?'*

I failed to add anything, just tried to look innocent.

'Er, Mum?' she asked. 'Is it, er, someone I might know, perhaps?'

'Well …' I settled back in the sofa: 'Someone you'd know *of*, yes.'

She said nothing, just looked at me; waited. 'Su A Kim,' is all I said.

THREE

THE INSTANT HE entered my office, ushered in by Anna, I knew I'd guessed right.

I'd told her to go for it. Dress for it. Prepare for the meeting with Ko Hyeon-gi as if it were an interview – because effectively that's what it was. I'd reasoned that it would be good practice – a rehearsal for interviews to come.

So she did go for it: figure-hugging blouse (two buttons undone); hair up; hint of mascara; suggestion of rouge; slash of red lippo (Central Line Scarlet, she called it. Pure *Mad Men*, I'd call it). And Ko's eyes almost popped their sockets.

And even though I'd made an effort too, by comparison, I looked pretty dowdy – that's if he even noticed me – which he didn't, until I coughed to catch his attention.

I stood up, shook his hand, offered him a seat – and Anna, as my dutiful assistant, offered him a tea. He said yes, but frankly I think he would have said yes to anything. Like a salivating St Bernard. I'm only surprised he didn't sit up and beg.

As Anna made the teas, in the section of my office optimistically called the kitchen, Ko and I small-talked about … well, small talk.

Anna came back with tea *and* biscuits (more generous than I), placed the tray down on my desk (cleavage) took a seat and we got down to business.

I hope I'm not making this all sound too flippant – Anna's knock-'em-dead look and Ko's tongue-lolling reaction – because it was far from frivolous. We were about to discuss a missing person case, possibly a murder. But the way people are, they way they react, is important to me. It's my job. And Ko, at that meeting, made me feel just a little bit uneasy. OK, men like good-looking girls. Or most do. But there's liking and there's liking. Too attentive, too slimy, not the kind of man I'd trust.

'And so,' he said, in a tone that was part charming, part patronizing, 'what can your very able assistant bring to the party?'

'Well, she's far better on the internet – her generation are, aren't they?'

Note: *her* generation, not *your* generation. Ko Hyeon-gi would probably put himself in Anna's age group. But despite boyish looks, he wasn't. He was a good fifteen years older. I wanted him to know I knew.

'Quite so,' he agreed. 'Will there be a large amount of research, then?'

'Most certainly,' I replied. 'We won't have access to police files, so we've got to do our own digging.'

Clearly this made sense because he nodded in agreement. Whether it mattered to him was another matter. I don't think he gave a damn about R&D. Just P&R.

'And don't forget,' I added, 'there'll be plenty of students to interview.' I leaned forward, picked up my tea and added pointedly: 'And Anna's *their* generation too.' Happy that I'd hammered home the point, I continued: 'You see, unlike the police, we've got no authority over anyone – we need to win them over or they'll just clam up.'

Again, he just nodded. Then he sat forward, stirred his tea (there was no sugar in it) and said: 'So that kind of begs the question of what you'll be doing. I mean, if your daughter is –'

'You can call me Anna,' interjected Anna.

'Ah, yes, well, if Anna's doing the research *and* doing the interviews …'

'Don't worry. I'll have plenty to do. Anyway, we'd be doing the interviews together.'

'Oh. Good cop, bad cop,' he laughed.

'We're both good,' I replied.

And that, negotiation-wise, meeting-wise, everything-wise, was pretty much that (we'd already discussed money over the phone – £1,500 to be divided between Anna and me). Which kind of confirmed my doubts.

After he'd left I asked Anna what she thought. Initially she came out with 'reasonably pleasant'. But that was only because she didn't want to jump right in there, all guns blazing. I'd purposely kept my counsel; wanted her opinion. But as we talked, quite predictably, she moved her assessment ever downward, starting with 'self-satisfied', followed by 'condescending' and eventually 'creepy'. When it came to judging character: like mother, like daughter.

'OK,' I said, 'I think it's about time I came clean.'

And come clean I did. Told her that, in my opinion, the whole thing was a sham. That we weren't supposed to catch anyone. Just look pretty.

'But Mum, that's outrageous! I thought you were a bloody feminist – back in the day, I mean. Women's rights, burning bras and stuff!'

'Feminist then, pragmatist now. Why destroy perfectly good underwear?'

'OK, but it doesn't mean you have to suck up to creeps like that.'

'I do what I have to.'

'What you *have to*! You're always telling me you're at an age where you can do what you want – you don't have to kowtow to anyone.'

'Look, Anna, if, by getting involved – assuming you want to get involved – we get this whole thing back in the public eye, and if it helps find Su A, then who cares? Who gives a damn *how* we achieve something? All that matters is that we *do*.'

I paused for a second; added a thought I'd hardly dared let

into my own mind: 'And what if we did come up with something? Wouldn't that be just wonderful ... if we two *women* actually proved them wrong?'

You know, there's a lot to be said for living at the bottom of a valley. Whichever way you go, the only way is up. I'm not sure Anna would necessarily agree, but over the years she's got used to my eccentric exercise habits.

I'd suggested we change into more comfortable clothes and walk up into Bromley for a coffee. Reluctantly, she'd agreed.

We didn't take the main road into the town centre, but hiked up the ever-rising, zig-zag path through Library Gardens, with its barren, wintry flower beds and occasional shivering squirrel, eventually finding our way out into the cold, depressing High Street. From there we quickly made it into The Glades shopping mall. No longer cold, no longer winter, no longer anything. Pedestrianized retail lobotomy.

We found a coffee shop. Not the Costa that Su A had last been seen in but the slightly steamier, British variety – grannies in raincoats, coffee in mugs – and settled down and talked.

'I just feel you should have a least told me why I was tarting myself up,' said Anna, pulling off her woollen gloves finger by finger.

'Hardly tarting yourself up. Dressing for an interview.'

'Yes, but you didn't say *why*.'

'For the reason people *always* dress up for an interview.' I shrugged. 'To get a job.'

'But you should have told me. I don't like secrets.'

'I promised I'd tell you, and now I have. And anyway, if I had told you, you wouldn't have agreed. I know you.'

'Precisely. I wouldn't have agreed. I had a right to know.'

I thought for a second. 'Look Anna, you're my daughter, right?' Obviously I didn't expect an answer – nor did I get one. 'Have you *any* idea what it's like, even the slightest? Can you *begin* to imagine what it's like losing your child? If I can do *anything* for her parents, I will. It's not the money, Anna. A half-decent divorce will earn me more than this case. And it's not the publicity thing either – yes, it could be nice, but I'm not that bothered. And if you think I'm contemplating all this just to give you an interest between jobs, think again. I'd just as soon sub you. I'm not doing this for you, or me, or that creep Ko. I'm doing this for a mother and a father.'

FOUR

THIS WAS ONE police job I didn't miss. Actually, that's not true. There were many police jobs I didn't miss. But meeting the parents of a deceased or missing child was way up there. The same helpless, empty, what-on-earth-to-say feeling I'd experienced many times before. Perhaps it wasn't quite so bad though because, in this case at least, I wasn't the first.

I played with the idea of saying something about being sorry, about how terrible it must be. But sorry and terrible are words they'd heard, and lived, a million times over. So in the end I didn't.

Mr and Mrs Kim, he in a dark suit and she in mauve, were dressed neatly, soberly, correctly. As we all were. But somehow, they looked faded. Their bodies, slim and upstanding, yet their souls – shivering in the winter wind – visibly drooping. Etched faces, hollowed eyes.

Having been introduced to them, Anna and I stood back. Despite everything, they remained a picture of respect. Reverence, almost. All but bowing to people they were introduced to. I wanted to scream. We, this yobbish, filthy Britain. This burn-the-shops-and-take-what-we-want culture. We had taken their daughter. Yet they remained totally and utterly respectful to us.

In attendance, on our side of the media scrum, apart from Anna and I, were Mr and Mrs Kim, Ko Hyeon-gi and Mrs Baker. Now Mrs Baker was – new terminology to me at the time – Su A's host mother. In the media, she had always been referred to as Su A's landlady. She wasn't. There's a world of difference. A world – an EFL *(English as a Foreign Language)* world – I would come to know during the coming months. She was just as crushed, just as destroyed, as Su A's real parents. Perhaps, if it were possible, even more so. Host mothers are, or should be, what they sound. Surrogate British mums. They cook, wash, acclimatize, and sometimes even love them as their own. Can you imagine how she felt? On top of all the other emotions – the love and the loss – she had guilt. Not just the guilt I felt as a British citizen, but in spades. A million compressing tons of it. Su A had disappeared from her care – on her watch. However illogical it seemed to you and me, she would feel that it was her fault. So it says loads, masses for Mr and Mrs Kim that they had asked her to this press conference. They, with all their other worries and arrangements: the booking, the packing, the flights from Seoul, even the clothes they were now standing in, were compassionate enough to realize that Doris Baker needed to be there too, if she wanted to be. And clearly she did.

So even though, outwardly, Mrs Baker was rosy cheeked and plump and would once have been as jovial as her Happy Families name suggested, she clearly wasn't now. And possibly wouldn't ever be again.

Conspicuous by their absence, to me anyway, were any members of Her Majesty's constabulary. Now, according to Ko Hyeon-gi – and I had no reason to disbelieve him – the police had been asked along. But they had declined, and this I could believe.

Think about it. They get asked to go to a press conference featuring the hiring of two private investigators, one an ex colleague and one a complete rookie. And even if we weren't, even if we'd been world experts on missing person cases, it would have been galling. Standing next to two private investigators, just off camera, given some minor role in a media event? It had 'police failure' written all over it.

Of course, not turning up wasn't a whole lot better either.

Some would construe it as not caring – or worse still, throwing in the towel. Beaten both ways.

I could picture my old boss, DCI Sullivan, the one person I really didn't miss from that place, absolutely seething. Teeth grindingly, pencil-snappingly furious. And I realized then, if I hadn't before, that Ko Hyeon-gi had pulled off an absolute masterstroke. Not only had he re-stoked up media interest in the case again, but he was putting massive pressure on the police. However hard they were working on it before, they'd have to work twice as hard now. Two aces from the same pack. Four if you included Anna and me. And the whole event had been stage managed to perfection too.

It could have taken place in central London, in a prestigious hotel, but it didn't. We could have had a purpose-built auditorium with a podium and microphones, but we didn't. Instead, he'd chosen an area just outside a shopping centre – with only its glass entry canopy protecting us from the spits and spats of winter raindrops – in boring, suburban Bromley, with us standing on what looked like a pallet from a builder's yard. But once you saw it from our angle, with the mêlée of press in front of us and the Market Square behind them, it was obvious. Why? You only had to think of the cameramen's POV. Right behind us and therefore framing us was a huge sign saying *The Glades*. But out and across the Market Square was the bus stop from which she'd made her final, fateful journey. Two doors from that was Costa Coffee, where she'd sipped a final coffee.

You could almost see the shot. Zoom out from Costa Coffee to the bus stop, pause, then pan across to us – at The Glades. Given that the police had never done a reconstruction of Su A's last movements (they would argue that it was a missing person, not murder) this was the next best thing. And if there were any doubts that this was precisely what Hyeon-gi was aiming at, the words that he asked me to sign off with – neatly typed onto windblown paper – said it all: '*If anyone can remember seeing anything that day, either in The Glades or the Market Square areas of*

Bromley, please don't hesitate to contact the police' (the police, note, not me). Reignite interest *and* pressurize the police.

So that's how we finished, with me gathering up my papers, thanking everybody, and extracting one final photo opportunity by shaking hands with Mr and Mrs Kim as I left the podium.

Prior to that, the questions had come thick and fast, the vast majority relating to police enquiries, leaving me no option but to give rather anodyne responses.

The most difficult question, unsurprisingly, came not from a local journalist but a seasoned Fleet Street hack, and related to Anna. *'I believe this is your daughter's first case, Ms Andrews?'* he said, looking up from his notepad. I was just about to answer this when Anna piped up: *'Erm, can I answer that, Mum?'*

Now I love Anna, but these occasions are minefields, even for the experienced. The last thing we needed was to kick off with a clever or inappropriate answer, especially when the only response to this was a simple 'yes'. But as she stepped up next to me (she was fully three inches taller in her heels) she said the opposite: *'No.'*

I froze. Was Anna stupid enough to broadcast a barefaced lie to the whole nation?

'No, you're wrong,' she repeated. My heart skipped a beat. 'You see, it's not my case. It's my mum's – and the police's, of course. I'm just helping - I hope.'

The sheer innocence of that answer brought a few smiles from the usually jaundiced hacks before us.

The media had their sweetheart.

FIVE

DAY ONE. SIMPLE plan. Anna stays in the office collecting and collating similar cases to Su A's and I'd be doing the leg work. Given the previous day's press conference had brought forth headlines like *'Mum & Daughter 'Tec Team To Find Sad Su'*, the police certainly wouldn't be offering too much help. So it was all down to the school. To this end I'd already made an appointment with the school's principal.

Standing in front of the mirror, buttoning up my coat, I gave Anna instructions as to the wheres and whens of my day ahead. But with her face already buried in the computer, all I got back was an absent minded 'Mm'.

I cut my losses and make for the door.

On my doorstep, something strange. I pick it up. Mistletoe. 'Kiss, kiss,' says the gift tag.

I go back to Anna – still glued to the screen – and ask if it means anything to her.

'No,' she says.

In the end we decide it's probably something to do with the teenage girl two doors down – you know, some secret admirer or something – and somebody's got the wrong house.

Anna says she'll deal with it – perhaps bin it, or drop it next door – and I leave the house for the second time.

From my little office in Shortlands, above the sawdust-and-guinea-pig-smelling shop below (oh, the glamour) it would have been a short journey to Su A's language school by car. But I decided to take the bus instead – *and* towards Bromley – the

opposite direction. The reason for this was that it would replicate part of the journey Su A and her student friends had taken
that fateful day. Having got to Bromley, I'd change buses and
double back on the 162 route. This would replicate the assumed
return leg – after she'd split with her friends.

I wanted to get the feel of those buses because, on this sort of
case, details are important. To most people this makes little
sense. After all, how could a little thing like sitting on a couple
of buses help? Well, for a start, when I interview her fellow
students (assuming I'd be permitted to interview her fellow
students) I want to be able to accurately visualize the setting.

Let's imagine, for instance, I'm speaking to a student about
their outward journey. I ask them where they sat. If they say
'Next to the doors' I can say: *'Do you mean the middle doors or the
doors near the driver?'* The importance of this sort of response is
not so much that I know my geography, but that *they* know I
know. For another example, let's take the return journey. As I
speak to the boy who allegedly took her final call (when she
screamed something about 'fortune tellers'), my knowledge of
his surrounding needs to be just as good as his. Then, given
enough questions (delivered casually, of course) I can look him
straight in his eye and, if he's lying, I'll know it. You see, as far
as questioning is concerned, the devil is in the detail.

Bus stop, wet day. The sky above was leaden, the people
below hatted and coated. Well, most of them. Standing next to
me, when I got to the stop, was a young, shivering girl in denim
hotpants, black leggings, skimpy top and bare midriff.
Seemingly, the only thing keeping her together was her body
piercings. Her boyfriend – if that's what they're called nowa-
days – was just as unseasonably dressed: cotton hoodie; jeans
round arse. Fashion? I'd rather be old than cold.

As the bus arrived, the boy got on before her, gobbing in the
gutter – such is modern etiquette – and I got on behind them. I
paid with a note – I don't quite qualify for a bus pass yet – which
the bus driver very grudgingly accepted. As he gave me my

change I noted a slight double take. Already, I was being recognized.

Like most things, this would have its pluses and minuses. On the plus side, because people knew who I was and what I was doing, they would open up (assuming they had sympathy for Su A) but on the other hand, if they had something to hide, they would clam up. But that's true of the police's position too. Overall, whether I liked the publicity or not, it was probably a good thing. At least it enabled me to pay a bus driver with a tenner.

The journey to Bromley Market Square took just minutes, first grinding up the steep hill from Shortlands, then edging right, into the narrow High Street. This gave me just enough time to stumble to the back of the bus – it was a single-decker – sit down and take a photo. When we got to the Market Square I got off, took a photo of the stop, walked to the 162, took another photo (rubbernecked by passers-by) and waited with a huddle of other souls, as buses came and went. I must have waited about fifteen minutes for a 162 – it was clearly a less frequent route. When it did come, it was also a single-decker, but smaller. Oh yes, and at least this time I had change for the fare.

On board, I sat down and took another photo. There was little for me to note. Like the bigger bus it had an illuminated sign telling us the next stop: *Bromley South Station.* It also had recorded announcements which told us its ultimate destination: *'162 ... to ... Beckenham Junction.'* I found myself wondering whether these automated functions were working when, and if, Su A got this bus. The only other thing worth noting was that one of the stops was called The Chinese Garage, which is a garage but not, by my reckoning, Chinese. If anything it's more Japanese or perhaps Korean in design. I assumed that this is no more than a coincidence and unconnected to Su A's disappearance. Could she have got off there out of sheer curiosity? Note duly made.

I alighted at its terminating point – Beckenham Junction

Station – and completed my journey with a brisk walk, through the wintry streets, to the college.

Kent House College is a large Victorian building with a few modern extensions tacked onto its sides. On a cold day such as this, it could have looked dour and institutional but, having recently had a lick of paint, and with winter pansies planted out into its forecourt beds, it didn't.

Just as I entered the front door, the end-of-lesson bell went and I found myself fighting against a tide of joyful, jabbering students. And as I stood aside, letting them pass, I made another mental note. Generally, it seemed a happy place. When the bell went, at least.

The reception, a large, high-ceilinged room, had been divided roughly down its centre by a long, hardwood counter. On the business side were three office staff, and on my side, a horde of question-asking students. The staff dealt with them patiently, one by one, until the room was clear enough for one of the reception staff, a pretty girl with dark curly hair and large Latin-looking eyes (magnified by glasses), noticed me. She apologized for keeping me waiting, but I told her not to worry. It was my fault for turning up at exactly the wrong time.

I noted that she had an Italian accent and that one of the other staff members, a tall, dark boy, sounded Spanish. The detective in me wondered if they were ex-students turned employees – a ready supply of multilingual staff.

I told her I had an appointment with Mr Taplow, the principal, and she asked me to take a seat. Up until then I hadn't even noticed there were any seats, so busy had it been in that area.

When he eventually came – hand outstretched in readiness – Edward Taplow looked every bit the academic. Tall, slightly stooped, with an angular face and horn-rimmed glasses – certainly striking, in a scholarly kind of way. He was well dressed too, though his once-expensive suit was a little baggy with wear, and shiny at the elbows – all adding to the slightly laissez-faire look, I suppose. Mostly, though, he was handsome. He reminded me of the Arthur Miller you see in 1950s photos, with a young, in-love Marilyn Monroe in his thrall. Intelligent, handsome, fatherly and kind-looking. Forgive my over-suspicious mind, but as I watched him, I found myself thinking what a potent mix – particularly if you're a lonely young girl in a strange country – that combination represented. But as I said earlier, that's probably just the detective in me.

He led me out of the reception, up a flight of reassuringly creaky stairs, onto a newly carpeted landing and then into his office.

With vaulted ceilings and quartz lighting, his office seemed very different to the Victorian fustiness of the rest of the building. Modern art, cool jazz playing softly in the background – very much the loft look. He was the boss, I suppose, so he could decorate his office as he wished. But everywhere else said old and this room said young. He was in his late fifties, but was that how he saw himself? Or was he, in his mind's eye, still young? As he ushered me in I checked his left hand. No wedding ring.

He closed the door behind us, offered me a chair, walked around his desk and sat down.

We talked about his business, then about my press conference, which he'd seen, until I eventually broached the main subject – the purpose of my visit.

'Mr Taplow,' I asked, 'as I mentioned on the phone, I really need a list of anyone who was in any way associated with Su A: classmates; friends; staff.'

'Yes,' he said, folding his arms, 'and as I mentioned, I'm not sure I can give you that.'

'Why?' I asked.

'Because it's confidential – the police have already been through all that.'

I paused for a second, trying to work out the best means of attack.

'Erm, Mr Taplow, may I ask you a question?'

'Of course, fire away.'

'Has the Su A case affected your business at all?'

'Most certainly, yes.' He noticeably relaxed, pleased to move onto a different subject, even if it was negative.

'So numbers are down a little?'

'Yes, though the European side – French, Italian – has held up well.'

'But Korean numbers are down?'

'Yes, and Japanese. And it's not only us. English schools across the country have reported reduced numbers. You can't really blame them, can you?'

'No, not at all,' I agreed. 'So it would be in your interests for the case to be brought to a close.'

'Of course! Everyone's interests, including her poor family.'

'Precisely, and it's her poor family who have hired me.'

'Yes, I know, but you have to look at it from the school's perspective ... raking all this up again ...'

'Mr Taplow, if I go back to Su A's parents, tell them you're being uncooperative, do you think it'll end there?'

'Uncooperative? We've been incredibly cooperative! We've helped the police and ...'

'I'm sure you have. But you haven't answered the question. Do you think Su A's parents will simply let it drop? They've flown over from Seoul, hired me, spent a fortune – do you think they'll just shrug their shoulders and walk away?'

'I suppose not, but ...'

'I'll tell you what Mr and Mrs Kim will do,' I said. 'They'll go straight to the press – particularly in their own country. How does the headline *"Su A's School Refuses To Help"* grab you?'

'But that's preposterous!' Flushed with anger, with nostrils flared, suddenly he didn't look so handsome. 'Are you threatening me, Ms Andrews?'

'No,' I replied calmly, 'I'm not. I'm simply telling you precisely what'll happen, that's all. If I walk away from here with nothing, I'm duty bound to tell the people hiring me. And if I were them, if my child had gone missing, that's precisely what I'd do. Mr Taplow, I'm not threatening anybody, I'm simply stating facts.'

I stood up and, buttoning my coat, said: 'Look, I don't mind if we do the interviewing here at the school. I fully understand that you don't want me chasing your students and staff around the country – they have a right to privacy, of course. And some people might not even want to be interviewed, that's also their right. But if you refuse me access to everyone at this school, you'll have to bear the consequences. It's that simple.'

I walked to the door, turned round and thanked him politely. I then made my way down the creaky stairs, smiled a goodbye to the Italian receptionist, left the school, crossed the road and waited at the bus stop.

It was starting to rain, so I huddled to the back of the shelter and looked up at the illuminated sign. Three minutes. Not too bad.

My mobile started to bleep so I fished it out of my bag. The word 'office' came up.

Office? What did that mean? Of course, as soon as I put the phone to my ear I realized. I'd never previously received a call from my own number because I normally worked alone. But this time, I wasn't.

'Hi, Anna, how's it going?'

'Hi, Mum, I, er, didn't know whether to call you or not.' I could hear anxiety in her voice.

'Are you OK?' I asked.

'Well, yes, but I've just had this really weird call.'

SIX

'I WAS SITTING at your desk and the phone rang,' said Anna, retreating to the office sofa. 'At first I didn't know whether to answer it. Then I thought, well, I'm working for you, so perhaps I should. I kind of wish I hadn't now – it would've gone to voicemail.'

'Tell me what he said again,' I said, as casually as I could – I really didn't want to spook her – adding further offhandedness by unbuttoning my coat and checking myself in the mirror.

'*"Which bitch are you?"* so then I said "sorry", you know, because I thought I might've misheard him. Then he said, *"You're the young one, aren't you? You're fucking next."*

'So I just put the phone down. Then I rang you.'

With my coat still unbuttoned, I sat down next to her and put my arm around her. 'Don't worry, Anna, it's only some silly crank. You often get them on cases like this.'

But do you? How would I bloody know? I hadn't had one single weirdo call during my entire police career (but police don't, do they?). And since going private, I'd only done divorces and surveillance. The nearest I'd got was one particularly nasty piece of work who came round and physically threatened me. But even that was different. At least he made no secret as to who he was.

After a few more words of comfort I got up, hung up my coat, made us both a cup of tea and sat back down with her again. As an investigator, what I should have done was pick up a pen and go over everything with her more carefully: accents, inflections, background noises – word for word, tone for tone, pause for pause. But as a mother I didn't. Like I said, I didn't want to make a big deal of it. So I brought up a few things about my own day, before slowly bringing the conversation back round to hers. And, nasty phone call apart, her day up to that point had, at the least, been pretty fruitful.

'I found thirty-nine women who've gone missing in the South East London area since 2008,' she said, flipping through her pad. 'And taking out those with other reasons – mental problems, sleeping rough etc. – you're left with just seven. Of those, none were language students but three were students of other kinds – and none went missing on buses – though one did disappear on a train.'

'Seven, you say?'

'Yes, just seven – and, oh, yes, not one of them from places like this – they all disappeared from inner London – you know, London Bridge, Lambeth. Squats and places like that – not one from suburbia.'

'Yes,' I said. 'That's why this one sticks out.'

'I suppose so,' she said, getting up and going to my desk. 'And I've been gathering stuff on them.'

She picked up some plastic files, walked back and gave them to me.

'Thanks,' I said, shuffling them.

She'd printed out web pages from missing persons sites, blogs, tweets and even local newspapers.

'Impressive,' I said. 'Bedtime reading.'

Noticeably, Anna had pulled up a chair rather than compressing herself next to me on the tiny sofa again. I took this as a sign that she was feeling more confident – the distance between us being positive.

'So,' I said, 'tell me about this idiot's phone call.'

Note: he was now just an idiot. Not dangerous, not even important. I still didn't write anything down either – just prompted her, listened, and kept notes in my head. I'd commit it to paper later. Then, as further questions arose, I'd bring them up – casually.

'Well, like I said, he simply said, *"Which bitch are you? You're the young one, aren't you? You're fucking next."*'

'That's all?'

'Yes. Then I put the phone down.'

'Have you tried 1471?'

'Doh!' she said, palming her forehead. 'How bloody stupid of me. Some detective!'

'No problem,' I said, getting up, walking to my desk, picking up the phone and dialling.

Completely against my expectation, the number wasn't withheld. *'Telephone number – 02085803373 – called – this afternoon – at one thirty-one hours … To return the call press three – there is normally a charge for this service.'*

I pressed the number three. It just rang and rang.

While it was ringing I found myself wondering. Just after 1.30. The caller's lunch break? A bit of Dutch courage before phoning?

Then, even more against my expectation, a man's voice answered: 'Hello.'

I hardly had time to gather my thoughts. 'Oh, er, hello. I was, er, wondering whether anyone had recently called this number.'

'No idea, love. This is a callbox.'

'A callbox?'

'Yeah.'

'Er, sorry, but you wouldn't mind telling me exactly where? Only I've just had a nuisance call and …'

'Kent House.'

'Near the college?'

'Yeah.'

'Thank you. Thank you very much.'

'No trouble.'

I put the phone down. Anna had taken my place on the sofa, curling herself up again. Possibly a comfort thing; sort of foetal.

'Where was it, Mum?'

'Kent House.'

'But that's …'

'Yes.'

Everything had changed. This was no coincidence. Not someone responding to our appearance on the news. This was from right next to the school. It could still just have been a crank caller, but if it was, it was a crank caller from nearby. Fellow student? Teacher? Staff member?

'Anna, do you remember anything about this man's speech?'

'Not really, no.'

I paused for a second.

'So he was English – or an English speaker?'

She bit her lip and thought. 'Well, if he was foreign, his English was certainly good.'

'Are you sure there was nothing?'

'Not really, no … well …'

While she continued to think, I said: 'Tell you what, Anna, let's re-enact it. I want you where you were sitting …'

'At the desk?'

'Yup. If that's where you were. I'll call you on my mobile – using the words you remembered – and you're going to answer it with your words.'

'OK,' she said, getting up and going over to my desk.

I followed, placing the files she'd made down in front of her.

'Try to remember what you were doing at the time.'

'I was on the internet.'

'Good, get back on it – and if you can remember the exact web page, all the better.'

As she was making herself comfortable at the desk, I opened one of the drawers and fished out a little hand-held Dictaphone. I then pressed 'record' and walked back to the sofa, placing it on the coffee table on the way.

Finally I sat back on the sofa, mobile in hand, while Anna found the website.

'That's it,' she said. 'South London Press – I was looking at something about a missing Nigerian girl.'

'OK, we almost have lift-off, but not quite. One more check.'

I got back off the sofa, went to the coffee table and rewound the tape. Very clearly it played Anna's voice: *That's it. South London Press – I was looking at something about a missing Nigerian girl*' followed by me: 'OK. *We almost have lift-off, but not quite. One more check.*' (Incidentally, I hate listening to my own voice back.)

'Good,' I said. 'Thunderbirds are go!'

'Sorry?'

'I said "Thunderbirds are go". That's Stone Age for "ready for action".'

'Oh,' she said, eyeing me doubtfully.

I cued up the tape again, sat back down, picked up my mobile, and pressed the ring sign.

The desk phone rang, Anna picked it up, and we acted it all out again.

'How similar?' I asked.

'Not,' she replied.

I had no intention of playing back the recording yet. Given that it wasn't similar, the fewer times she heard it the better. It would simply wipe out the original memory.

'In what way?'

'Well, for a start, he was a man and you're my mum.'

'Well, yes, *obviously*.' There was clearly still some work to be done on Anna's detective skills.

'But even without that,' she said, smiling, 'he was more, well … sort of menacing.'

'In what way?'

She thought for a while. 'Can I hear it back?'

'Not yet,' I replied. 'Just think.'

Looking away from me, she thought some more, nearly saying something – then thinking again. 'OK, I might have it. You had more up-and-down in your voice, more expression.'

'Intonation,' I said.

'Yes, more intonation.'

'Good. Anything else?'

'There is something, but I can't quite put my finger on it – are you sure I can't hear it back?'

'I'd rather you didn't. Not unless you really have to.'

She mumbled it back to herself a few times. 'Um, I think I know what it could be – but I would like to hear it again – just for confirmation.'

'OK.' I got up, rewound the tape and played it again.

'Yes.' She nodded. 'That's it.'

'That's what?'

'Well, you said: *"You're the young one, aren't you? You're fucking next"* and he said: *"You are the young one, aren't you? You are fucking next."* You said *"you're"* and he said *"you are"*.

'Are you sure?'

'Positive.'

I thought for a second: 'Do you think he said it for emphasis? You know: *"You are the young one, aren't you? You are fucking next."'*

'No, definitely not – I would've remembered it – it doesn't even sound right.'

She was right, it didn't sound right. If you were going to emphasize anything it would probably be "fucking", as in: *"You're fucking next."'*

'Could he have been foreign then?'

'Possibly, but if he was, his English was very good – definitely not a strong accent.'

And we kind of left it at that. I didn't want to go on and on about it for a number of reasons. Firstly, I didn't want to worry her any more than was necessary. Secondly, playing a tape of my voice over and over again, forcing her into thinking it was a particular accent, wouldn't help. She'd made her decision.

Time was already getting on, so we shut up shop and took the short walk home. This involved skirting the edge of the rec and, if you're in that frame of mind, it can be a little spooky – a pitch-black park to the left, a tall brick wall, hemming us in to the right.

The only further mention I made of the whole episode was to tell her that I would definitely have to get DCI Sullivan, my old boss, involved. There were plenty of reasons not to. One: I disliked him. Two: he'd give me a hard time about my involvement – I was only surprised he hadn't already called. Three: he'd relish the fact that I had come crawling to him for help. But I still had to contact him. I'd promised Su A's parents that if anything came up I would contact the police. Already, something had.

And there was another reason: Anna. If this guy did turn out to be a threat, I would never forgive myself.

I spent the evening going over Anna's files whilst she, back on her old stamping ground, went out for a drink with a few of her old mates. I suppose I would have liked her to stay in, but I wasn't about to suggest it. It would've rather blown the whole nonchalance thing.

So I waved her off at eight (not literally, me standing at the front door would have been a bit of a giveaway), settled down and tried to concentrate – but soon found myself looking at the clock, wondering, worrying, waiting.

In the end, as promised, she arrived home at eleven, escorted to the front gate by a lad who lives just up the road. Not that I was standing by the curtains and checking or anything.

'Hiya, Mum,' she (slightly) slurred. 'No attackers tonight.'

She then stumbled her way up the stairs and disappeared into the loo for an unnaturally long pee.

Funny, isn't it. Worry about her living in New Cross, worry about her *not* living in New Cross. Worry about her working in Soho, worry about her *not* working in Soho. Worry about her having boyfriends, worry about her *not* having boyfriends. Worry about her doing homework, worry about her *not* doing homework. And even when she was a new born baby in her cot, worry when she cried, worry when she didn't. Back and back. Worry, worry.

SEVEN

THERE WERE MANY good things about having Anna about the house, but getting her up in the morning after she'd had a few drinks wasn't one of them. By the time I'd coaxed her from her bed, directed her to the bathroom and bundled her (unbreakfasted, partially dressed) into the car, I was about forty-five minutes late. And by the time I'd driven to the office (passenger mirror down, unsteadily applying make-up), driven round and round for a parking space (leaning back again, eyes closed, feeling sick) and hurried to the office (forty paces behind), it had become a full hour.

Once inside, while Anna flopped onto the sofa, I buzzed about opening blinds, switching on the computer, checking the voicemail and putting on the kettle.

My inbox didn't throw up what I was hoping for – no email from Edward Taplow waving the white flag – but did contain a message from Hyeon-gi asking if I was free for a meeting. I had no idea what he wanted to talk about, but one thing was for sure – I'd be listening out for his pronunciation. From memory it was near perfect – if a little expressionless and monotone. But did he say 'you are' rather than 'you're'?

I was also half expecting a call from a certain Detective Chief Inspector Sullivan. He would be fuming – and he wasn't the kind of man to bottle it up. But nothing from him either.

My first call was one I wasn't looking forward to – there again, in this sort of business, there are loads of calls and meetings you don't look forward to. Having pored over Anna's missing persons' files, one stood out – a girl called Rachel Baimbridge. Unlike most of the other girls in the file, she wasn't a runaway, wasn't a rough sleeper, didn't have a drug or drink problem and wasn't even associated with any iffy people. And like Su A she was a student, was in her early twenties and had disappeared on public transport (a train from London Bridge). And even though she didn't come from this exact locality, she did at least have connections around here – her family was from Biggin Hill.

There was one other reason why I wanted to look into the Rachel incident first though. When I was in the Met I was briefly involved in her case – having even interviewed her mother. I already had all her details, right down to her mum's phone number, so hopefully I didn't need any further research from Anna – which was fortunate because, even though she had finally stirred herself from the sofa, it was simply to go down to the local sandwich shop. I was beginning to have grave doubts about the workability of this particular mother-daughter partnership.

I called the number I had and, when a female voice answered, I immediately recognized it as Mrs Baimbridge. It wasn't just the age in her voice (she would now be over seventy) but the loss. Not just the unsteadiness, but the emptiness of losing a child.

I apologized for disturbing her, told her of my business – she did remember me from years gone by, and had also seen me in the papers – then arranged to meet her in about hour. Oh yes, and I made sure she wasn't under the illusion I had any news about Rachel. In these cases, hope can be crueller than hopelessness.

With my working day finally up and running, next was DCI Sullivan. Unfortunately he wasn't available and though I could have – and officially should have – spoken to a lesser mortal, there would have been no point. It would all end up in his lap anyway. So I left a message asking if we could meet up later in the day. My guess was that he'd jump at the chance. Laying into me would be too tempting to resist.

I left Anna to her egg and bacon sarnie, instructing her to spend the morning making my office look a little more like an incident room – wall photos, maps, etc. – because of Sullivan's impending visit. And when that was done, she could ruddy well get back on the computer – and she'd better not get bacon grease all over my keyboard either!

Biggin Hill is one of those strung-out, semi-rural communities of bungalows and semis, with nothing much to commend it – apart from its once-famous Battle of Britain aerodrome. This is marked, at the beginning of the town, by the roadside carcasses of two fighter planes – a Spitfire and a Hurricane – stuck on spikes, like the heads of dead warriors. Just past these lifeless husks, and just before the main street, I took a left down a country lane bounded by leafless, winter hedgerows and the occasional rundown cottage. Driving slowly and peering through gates, I eventually came across *Lark View*, one of two squeezed-together pebble-dashed semis (how strange are isolated semis) which, despite their lateral meanness, had long, straight driveways. I drove up the drive – manicured lawn to my left, all-important dividing fence to my right – until I reached the house, pulling up next to an ancient Citroen. I got out, walked to the door – stained glass, metal 'lark' knocker – and rang the inappropriately cheerful door chimes.

Mrs Baimbridge soon appeared, unbolting various locks and chains from the inside, and greeted me kindly. Despite being relatively short, she had broad shoulders and a big face. In fact, even given her sack-like floral dress, her overall appearance was rather masculine – a sort of stocky, sad Mrs Doubtfire.

She directed me to the front parlour – Royal Doulton figurines, cut-glass crystal – and I waited for the inevitable cup of tea. Like the semis themselves, the chintziness of my surroundings seemed all the more incongruous for being isolated in windblown fields.

She came back in with not just tea, but biscuits, putting her tray down on the coffee table between us and settling back into the chair opposite. I apologized, yet again, but she deflected my apologies, saying it was good to have company – she had so few visitors. It was at this point that I realized she had said 'I', not 'we'. Thinking back, there never was a Mr Baimbridge.

The loss of a child, without so much as a funeral, is a terrible thing – and I found it a difficult subject to broach. The easiest way (if that's the right word) would have been to direct our attention towards a photo of her daughter, via a nod, a turn of the head, or even by getting up and going over to it – I know it's cowardly, but I've found that looking away from the interviewee helps when you bring up such subjects. But there were no photos. This really did surprise me. There again, everyone has their own way of dealing with grief.

I didn't find out much that I didn't already know about Rachel's disappearance. Mrs Baimbridge supported the theory that her daughter was spending that Saturday researching her degree thesis (family life during World War II) and was making her way from her Bermondsey flat to the Imperial War Museum when she disappeared. Her great regret – one that would clearly haunt her forever – was that this was a last-minute change of plan. This was news to me.

'Yes,' she sighed, looking down at her cold tea: 'She was going to come home that weekend, you know, originally.'

I looked at her; didn't say anything.

'She changed her mind. There was this exhibition on in London, so she went to that instead.'

After a longish silence, and for want of something to say, I asked: 'Did she come home often?'

'No, not really. You see, she had so much going on. Friends and stuff. I didn't mind. The most important thing was she was happy.'

An even longer silence followed, so in the end I just said: 'Was there something special?'

'Special?'

'Yes, that weekend. You said she didn't normally come home.'

'Oh, well, no, not really. She was going to do some stuff locally – you know, research on the war – and tie it in with coming home.'

The conversation became pretty vague after that, so I didn't push her much further.

From recollection, the exhibition at the War Museum she allegedly went to was all about life in the Blitz – Anderson shelters, ARP wardens and that sort of thing – and I couldn't think of anything like that round here. And anyway, it was the first time I'd heard this theory – something she'd come up with since my original enquiry. It was possible that the idea of her daughter coming home that weekend was just something she'd built up in her head.

Driving back to Shortlands, via traffic-choked Bromley, something struck me. Why, if Rachel was travelling from Bermondsey to Lambeth, where the Imperial War Museum is, would Rachel have been going by Tube? Visualizing the Underground map – I had developed a good copper's memory of it – that would involve a walk from her flat to London Bridge, the opposite direction to the Imperial War Museum, then one stop south to the Elephant (Northern Line) then one stop north to Lambeth (Bakerloo) then another walk south. Now that's the kind of thing tourists do – take the Tube map literally. But Londoners – at least, those with legs and brains – know differently. Frankly, Rachel could have walked it in fifteen minutes, or bussed it in ten.

So given that Rachel was definitely at London Bridge concourse when she disappeared, as the CCTV footage clearly showed, where else could she have been going? The mainline station, maybe? And where do the trains from London Bridge go to? The Bromley area. So maybe Rachel had been coming home after all. But where, if that was the case, would her 'local research' on WWII have been?

When I got back my office had been totally transformed and

I found myself feeling guilty for being cross with Anna earlier. Neatly pinned to the wall, and immediately apparent as you walked in, was a large local map. Traced out on it, in highlighter pink, was the direct route Su A had taken from Kent House to Bromley. And in highlighter yellow, the (possible) return journey on the 162. Marker pins pinpointed all the strategic points – host family, school, entrance to Glades Shopping Centre, boarding point, and (possible alighting) point. Around the edges were various pictures – digital photos I'd taken of bus stops and bus interiors, blurred stills taken from CCTV footage, the smiling Su A featured in the tabloids, a group photo of her friends. All very professional – and perhaps a little poignant given the visit I'd just made.

'Fantastic!' I said, putting my bag down and taking off my coat. 'Great job!'

'Thanks. I've kind of copied the way I've seen it on TV.'

I'd like to have said that I gathered that, due to the one rather over-theatrical touch. On a scrap of paper above the map she had added the single word 'Mudang' – Su A's alleged final word. That would certainly have to come down if Sullivan were coming round. I was going to have to find a diplomatic way of explaining to Anna that we're supposed to be dealing with proven facts, not tabloid fiction.

I hung up my coat and walked over to Anna, who was still glued to my computer screen.

'How you feeling now?'

'Oh,' she said, rather absentmindedly (Anna plus computer: another universe). 'I'm, er, OK.'

Then she paused, thought and, still looking at the screen, added: 'Good news.'

'What's that?'

'The school have agreed to let us see their records – providing we do the interviews there.'

'That *is* good news,' I said, as she quit a web page and went into my email (note *my* email) to show me the message from

Edward Taplow (I'd like to have asked her where she got my password from, but hey ho).

'And another piece of good news,' she said. 'At least I think it is.'

'What's that?'

'DCI Sullivan called.'

'Did he indeed?'

'Said he could do a meeting at four.'

Not a bad morning – and an interesting afternoon ahead.

EIGHT

HYEON-GI'S REASON for visiting me wasn't particularly apparent. Especially given he was over twenty minutes late. Having accepted a glass of water from Anna, he hung up his coat, lounged back on the sofa (requiring Anna to pull up a chair next to me at my desk) and talked about nothing in particular, except himself. I found myself wondering if he'd ever get to the point – assuming he had one.

And as per our previous encounters, but now even more so, he was coming over as a little too familiar for my liking. If Anna had remained squeezed up next to him on the sofa – which thankfully she wasn't – he'd probably have taken the opportunity to crack some crap joke and slap her on the knee. I got the uncomfortable feeling he felt he owned us; bought us with Mr and Mrs Kim's money.

After a bit, his mission – apart from sidling up to Anna – became a little more apparent. It seemed that Su A's parents were flying back to Seoul and he wondered if we could be at Heathrow to see them off. And surprise, surprise, a local journalist, plus someone from Radio London, would be there too. So the purpose of his visit was, predictably, the same as ever: photo opportunity dressed up as mercy mission. I did still have sympathy for Mr and Mrs Kim's plight, of course, but no longer had the time. Having said that, I was happy to listen – not to what he said, but the way he said it.

So did he have a slight accent? Yes. Would Anna have missed it on the phone? Possibly; after all, it was a nasty call. And flat intonation? Again, yes. So what about the main point: did he tend towards 'you are' rather than 'you're'? Yes, sometimes, and unlike a native speaker it wasn't solely for emphasis – more to do with preciseness. So could he have been the man behind the call? Only Anna could answer that.

But if it was him, he certainly had some front. Threatening call one day, cosy meeting the next.

On the photo opportunity front, I pointed out to him, in the most diplomatic way I could, that he either wanted us to work on this case or he didn't. Frankly, our list of meetings was building up and with half the school to get through we were way too busy.

So I came up with a plan B. He'd go to Heathrow to gladhand the Kims in front of the press – but only after he'd photographed us in front of Anna's incident-room mock-up.

This idea he loved – giving him the added bonus of physical contact with Anna: adjusting shoulders, lifting chin, moving a stray lock of blonde hair from her face.

'Just perfect,' he proclaimed.

Yes, Ko, I bet it was.

That's when everything changed. Once this 'perfect' photo had been taken, I happened to mention that I had a meeting coming up with Sullivan and his nonchalance evaporated. I got the distinct impression he didn't want to be around when the police turned up. Did he have something to hide?

Once he had gone, there was a good ten minutes before Sullivan turned up. Time for a coffee and a debriefing:

'OK,' I said, settling back into the sofa (Anna was perched on its arm, looking thoughtful). 'What did you think?'

'Ugh,' she shuddered.

'Yes, but I meant his voice.'

'Ah, right, yes.' She nodded. 'Could've been him.'

'You noticed he said "I am meeting Mrs Kim"?'

'Yes, but not always. He also said "I've got the press there" not "I have got the press there".'

'Mm, I got that too.'

'So he kind of mixes the two. But it certainly could've been him.'

She then got up off the sofa's arm and went back to my desk, moving my computer screen away to enable her to look straight at me.

'But what I don't understand is why. Why would he even do it? And if he was involved, why would he be helping Su A's parents to find her?'

'That's far more common than you would imagine, Anna. Murderers are often found helping the police, mingling with the press, getting involved. They get some kind of kick from it – or perhaps think it's the best form of cover. And we've found out something else about Hyeon-gi.'

'What's that?'

'He knew her before she disappeared. If the Kims had contacted him out of the blue, after she'd disappeared, it would've been way too coincidental – he'd be pretty well in the clear.'

'That's why you asked him about what he did before he came to London.'

'Exactly – used to work for Mr Kim in Seoul. He would have known Su A as a child. Friendly old Uncle Ko, here to meet her in the UK.'

'Do you think the police know about him?'

The answer to that question was just walking up our stairs, almost as we spoke.

DCI David Sullivan had enough presence, size-wise, to fill any room – especially my little office. Visually, he would've made a perfect northern, working men's comic: ruddy faced, wide girthed and narrow minded. Except he was neither northern nor comic. Frankly, we saw eye to eye on just one thing. I disliked him. He disliked me.

Of course, some would disagree with that. After all, you can't survive for twenty-five years in the force on bullying alone. And you can't get to the rank of detective chief inspector without some redeeming features. So a sizable number of policemen might differ. There again, a sizable number of policemen are just that … police*men.*

Having been politely welcomed in by Anna, his first comment, on seeing her handiwork on the wall opposite was 'Been watching too many TV detectives, have we?' (Thank God I'd removed the *Mudang.*) And then, as Anna offered him a tea (he sitting his fat arse down on the exact spot she'd just vacated), he patronizingly replied: 'Yes, dear.'

I was immediately reminded why I had taken early retirement.

His next comment, the hilarious 'What can I do you for?', got my response: 'We've had a nuisance call.' To which he said: 'Me too – which is why I'm here, ha ha.'

On this case, DCI Sullivan was clearly going to be in full-blown arsehole mode.

'Look, David,' I said. 'If you're not going to take this seriously …'

'Seriously?' he said, raising his voice. 'I'll give you seriously. You demoralizing my team, you poncing about on TV – that's what's serious. How the fuck do you think all that's going to help?'

'Well,' I said, giving his question more consideration than it deserved, 'it gets her back in the public eye.'

'Oh right,' he said, nodding knowingly. 'At least you've picked that up. At least you've got the sense to realize what you've been hired for.'

'I would imagine,' I said, 'I've been hired for the same reason as you – to help find Su A.'

'Not strictly true,' he replied, shaking his head. 'I'm here because you rang me. Now, what do you want? I'm a busy man.'

With impeccable timing Anna re-entered – tea in one hand, sugar bowl in the other – and politely asked: 'Sugar, David?' (He hated 'David'. His working name was 'sir'.)

'Two sugars,' he grumbled.

She put his tea down, spooned in the sugar, stirred it thoroughly, said, 'There you are,' and calmly walked away.

'So you're not interested in threatening phone calls – relating to the Su A case, I mean.'

'I didn't say that,' he replied, 'but you know as well as I do there are ways and means. I'm not taking your statements – I'll get a couple of the lads down.'

'Fair enough, but as you're here – to bawl me out, it seems – are you interested, at least, in hearing what happened?'

All I got from that was a shrug. So with Anna sitting down next to me, I went through everything carefully, clearly, chronologically.

'Well,' he said, 'That's exactly what you're going to get, isn't it? Every fruitcake in the vicinity giving you a courtesy call.'

'So that's what you think – it's just a nuisance caller?'

'Yes, but like I said, I'll get someone down to deal with it.'

'And put a tracer on my phone?'

'After one miserable call? We have got other cases on, you know.'

Having got nowhere on that, I decided to move on. 'Look, David, when I took this on it was with grave misgivings. I didn't want to work against you – I wanted to work with you. I'm not in this for the glory – I genuinely want to help.'

'Funny way of showing it.'

'OK, that's your opinion. But think about it – if I wasn't doing this, someone else would be. Someone who doesn't give a shit about you lot.'

I got no response to that. He presumably didn't give a shit about his lot either.

I pressed on. 'And I've promised Su A's parents I'll pass on any information I get. And on that subject, I've got a name that might interest you – Korean guy – Ko Hyeon-gi.'

'What have you got on him?' he said, slightly more interested.

'In truth, nothing – except he could be the caller …'

'I'm not certain it was his voice, Mum,' said Anna.

'I know that. But there's nothing to stop him being interviewed, is there, David?'

'Depends,' said Sullivan, shrugging. 'As long as there's a reason, some kind of connection.'

'Oh, there's a connection all right. He's the guy in the background in press conferences.'

Sullivan just nodded.

'Ah, so you haven't interviewed him yet?' I smiled.

'I didn't say that,' he replied. But he knew I'd got him. Hyeon-gi had slipped their net.

Just forty-eight hours in and I'd supplied them my first name. Not that he appreciated it.

NINE

THE NEXT FEW days went well, but produced little. Every day I'd open up the office, check my mail then drive over to the school to do interviews, leaving Anna to hold the fort. There were a couple of minor variations to this. On the Monday, I also checked out the phonebox. As expected, it revealed nothing (coins only, no CCTV nearby) except perhaps that the local population used it as a toilet. I'd already assumed that the caller wouldn't have used plastic (though Sullivan wouldn't have authorized a check anyway) so phonebox-wise, that was that.

The only other variation was on Tuesday. In the morning Anna accompanied me to the school and sat in on my interviews. I thought this would be good for her – one day she may have to stand in for me. Oh yes, two policemen, PCs Wilkins and Pollard, came round to take statements about nuisance calls (their description) but given the time between my reporting of it and their appearance (two days) I didn't hold out much hope.

The interviews were going reasonably well. I was obviously restricting myself to students who were at the school at the time of Su A's disappearance, but separating them out was more complicated than it sounds. This was because the school operated what they called continuous enrolment. This entailed newcomers on a Monday, leavers on a Friday and frequent changes to and from different language levels as their English improved. To add to this, Su A had two sets of classmates: morning classes for general English and afternoon classes for IELTS. But by carefully going over the school's records I was able to identify all her ex-classmates, plus teachers – over sixty interviews in total, and far more than the police would have interviewed. Quite an arduous task, especially in the small, windowless box room I'd been allocated, but I felt I had to go that extra mile.

By keeping the interviews short (fifteen minutes max), by Thursday evening we'd completed almost a third of them. Not bad for an eye-candy daughter and a sell-by candy Mum.

Pretty much everyone confirmed that Su A was a shy, quiet girl (teachers adding words like studious, punctual, hard-working) and certainly not someone who would just up sticks and run. However, there were just a few interviewees that begged to differ, even if only slightly.

The first person to hint that anything even vaguely untoward could have been going on was also one of the first people I'd ever noticed at the school – when I was sitting in the reception waiting to see the principal. His name was Eduardo, the male half of the receptionist duo.

Extending a hand and smiling, Eduardo Lopez made my shabby little interview room look immediately brighter, if smaller. He pulled up a chair – me surrounded by box-files and books, he framed by the door (awkward to re-shut once someone had entered) – and told me how pleased he was to meet me. Some of the younger people at the school – both staff and pupils – were already treating us like celebrities; such is the power of a fleeting TV appearance.

After the pleasantries, Eduardo told me all about himself. Twenty-four years of age, originally having come over here to improve his English (I'd guessed that bit) and then, having gained a CAE, had been offered a job at the school and stayed on. He'd been there since the previous summer and lived in a flatshare in Crystal Palace.

As a receptionist, especially in a language school, he was just perfect. Apart from his good looks and his charm, he was both knowledgeable and multilingual. He was also, more pertinently, in a very good position to judge Su A's movements. All excursions were booked through him and he could list all her daytrips (Oxford, Brighton, Bath), shows (*We Will Rock You, The Lion King*) and visits (Madame Tussauds, London Eye). He also knew the people she hung out with, and when I asked him about her friends he came up with the same half-dozen names everyone else had.

But then he paused and I caught a slight look in his eye – a tiny flicker that seemed to say *there's something else.* In the brief silence that followed, I asked him straight: 'Is there anything else, Eduardo?'

'Pardon, madam?'

'To do with her friends, maybe?'

'No, no,' he replied, perhaps slightly flustered. 'Just those names I've given you.'

That wasn't what I'd asked him. I hadn't asked if she had any further friends, I'd asked if there was anything further *relating* to those friends. But he simply re-listed them, this time on his fingers: 'Yoomi, Nadija, Arman, Viktor, Carlos … Chen.'

Was that final pause significant? Chen was the boy who'd received her mudang call. Was he somehow emphasizing it?

Subtly, I pressed him on this as much as I could. But no. He simply suggested I talk to them myself – which of course, I would.

Another interview of note was with a supply teacher and occasional lecturer called Albert Christopher. I had no particular reason to suspect him of anything: he had a good alibi for that Saturday – watching a football match with his mates.

Unlike Eduardo, he was anything but scrummy on the looks front: overweight, fifty-something and so unfashionable he was almost back in vogue again – big collar and tanktop. Mind you, I can't see his Bobby Charlton comb-over coming back into fashion any time soon. He did come up with some really useful information, though – jovially (too jovially?) handing over a list of all the students who had attended his lecture that week, of which Su A had been one.

It turned out that the school ran a diploma course, and part of the qualification process involved attending a given number of lectures. For this reason, at the end of each talk, students had to sign their name on a form. This was well worth knowing because Su A had attended all three lectures that week and all those attending would now be traceable. No one else at the school had thought to mention this. Well done, Albert!

The form he pushed across to me (*Ancient Britain: its Language, its Customs – A Lecture by Albert Christopher*) had twenty-six names on it. Two-thirds of the way down was the neatest of little signatures, *Su A Kim*. Just looking at the tiny, child-like letters almost brought a lump to my throat.

Perhaps the only downside was that I made the mistake of asking him about his talk – yielding a ten-minute verbal pasting about Druids, Saxons and God knows what else – even as I was trying to usher him out of the door. Nice guy, though.

Oh yes, and it also became apparent that he had both a young family and another on the way. It never ceases to amaze me how men do it. Christopher's wife would have to be, at the very least, ten years his junior – twenty, probably. Could I, at my age, attract a young man of child-bearing (so to speak) age? Would I even want to? And why do women do it? He was no great catch – an overweight, balding supply teacher. I couldn't help thinking that Mrs Christopher could have done just a tiny bit better. There again, who was I, a middle-aged, on-the-shelf divorcee, to judge?

Mind you, at least he was open, happy and helpful. Which is more than can be said of my next interviewee.

Paul Farrell conformed to one of my pet hates – a scruffy teacher. Call me old-fashioned but I've always thought that teachers should be on the smart side of casual, at least. Turn-ups, tweed jackets, elbow patches – that sort of thing. John Alderton from *Please Sir!*, for instance.

Farrell looked absolutely nothing like John Alderton from

Please Sir! Worse still, he appeared to favour what I'm given to believe is Nu Metal/Iron Goth apparel. Not ridiculously so – no visible piercings – but enough. Black featured heavily, as did T-shirts with obscure, chalky-white motifs on them. Worst of all, though (yes, it gets worse), he had a ponytail. I hate ponytails. Pathologically. They're passable on young men, OK on teenage girls – and absolutely essential on ponies. But on middle-aged men? No thanks.

Don't get me wrong, Farrell wasn't smelly or anything. His jeans and trainers were vaguely sanitary, and his T-shirt (with a pentangle on it) had even been ironed – at some stage, anyway. He might even have washed his hair once. But you kind of knew that, given half a chance (probably on Saturdays) he'd scruff himself up, put on some ridiculously loud music and play air guitar in front of his Jack Daniels mirror. And you also knew that he probably did, somewhere about his body, have a piercing or two. Imagining exactly where made me physically shudder.

The timetables I had in front of me suggested that his final contact with Su A should have been a Thursday afternoon (therefore a two-day gap before her disappearance). However, during the course of the interview, I discovered that he'd had contact with her after that. I wouldn't say I had to push him for this – he wasn't evasive. But he wasn't exactly helpful either.

'So the last time you taught her would have been on the Thursday afternoon?'

'Yeah.'

He lounged back, putting his nicotine-stained fingers (roll-ups? joints?) to his chin.

'And that's the last time you saw her?'

He thought for a bit (like he needed to – he was bound to have been asked this before), then answered: 'Possibly.'

'Possibly?'

'Well, I might have seen her on the Friday evening – for the lecture.'

'Ah, you too.'

'Me too, what?'

'Well, I've just interviewed Albert Christopher and he gave the lecture on the Wednesday.'

'Good for him.'

(He was beginning to annoy me.)

'And you were at the lecture on the Friday?'

'No.'

'You just said …'

'I wasn't *at* the lecture, I *gave* it.'

'Right – you *gave* the lecture – and Su A was there?'

'Like I said, possibly.'

'Mr Christopher was able to give me a list of everyone at his lecture,' I said, picking up the photocopied form.

'Again, good for him.'

'You wouldn't have a similar list, I suppose?'

'No. I gave it in. Ask the school.'

'You didn't make a copy?'

'No.'

'OK, for the minute, let's assume she definitely was there. What time would this have been?'

'Couldn't say when she got there, but lectures are at eight.'

'Were there many others?'

'Other what?'

'Students, Mr Farrell. Were there many other students?'

'Yes, it was full. My lectures are always full.'

I drew breath; considered the modesty of this statement.

'And what was the subject?'

'Legends, Myths and Magic.'

Again I paused. I suppose I hadn't expected such a topic in an English school.

'Is that, er, normal?'

'Normal?' he said, looking at me as if I was an idiot. 'Yes, of course it's normal.'

I was to find out later, when interviewing Taplow, the principal, that about fifty per cent (as per Farrell's) were simply interesting subjects (though vaguely English based) and fifty per cent linguistic.

'Did you speak to her?'

'Yes, I spoke to everyone. I was the lecturer.'

(Oh, very clever.)

'No, I mean *specifically*. Did you speak *specifically* to her, at any time?'

'No. I just left.'

'So you don't know where she went?'

'Not at the time, no. But I'm told she went with others, to the pub.'

'The pub – that's The George, isn't it?'

'I'm told so, yes.'

'And what did you do?'

'Went home.'

'By yourself?'

'Yes, by myself.'

'And what did you do the following morning?'

'Look, what is this?'

'It's an interview, Mr Farrell.' (I too can be clever.)

He thought for a bit before answering: 'Why should I tell you? I've already told the police.'

I just looked at him; bought myself some time.

'I'm assuming you have. But I'm not the police, I'm just trying to help. It's up to you what you tell me.'

'OK, I went to Croydon.'

'To do what?'

'Shop.'

'With?'

'My kids. Picked them up from their mum's.'

'And you've told all this to the police?'

'Yes, I've told all this to the police.'

In the end I just let him slouch away. I'd later find out that about half of what he'd told me was an outright lie. And it would be the following week, when interviewing Chen Choi, before I'd find out just how significant those lies were.

TEN

FRIDAY MORNING, A full week of interviews behind us. Most interviewees already had pictures in their head of Su A and what happened to her – just regurgitating what the media had told them. I was finding it hard separating the stories of those who possibly knew something from the stories of those who just thought they did. Speculation had become recollection; recollection, conviction.

So what did we actually have in the way of leads? A very tenuous connection with the earlier disappearance of Rachel Baimbridge, a hint that Su A might have had something going on with Chen, and a few misgivings about a teacher called Paul Farrell – mainly based on the fact that he wore black T-shirts!

Behind me, reflected in the hall mirror as I readied myself for work – pursing lips and straightening cuffs – appeared Anna, still in her pyjamas, pecking at a yogurt, having wandered from the kitchen fridge.

'Morning,' she said.

'Morning, sleepy-head,' I replied.

Her reflection dropped behind the back of the lounge sofa.

We'd already agreed that she could go into the office a bit later and generally have an easier day. For my part, I only had two interviews left for the week – Mrs Baker and Mr Taplow – both of whom I'd met before.

'Doing anything this weekend?' I asked, still considering my reflected image.

'Nothing much,' she yawned.

I hoped I wasn't being too nosey, but I suppose I was still a little concerned about that threatening phone call. So I went into the lounge, busying myself by pulling open blinds, shedding slatted sunlight on Anna, and picking up last night's wine glasses and twice-read magazines, whilst gently enquiring further:

'So what's nothing much?'

'Well, nothing, really. Don't think I'm not going out on Saturday.'

'How about tonight?'

No answer. Interesting. Not like Anna.

I focused on her reflected image. She was fiddling with her mobile phone. The period of time between my question and her non-answer lengthened. I suppose she could have answered, 'Oh, just something,' but that would be worse – telling me even more than silence. Poor girl. Fancy having a detective for a mum.

Anna yawned yet again (genuine tiredness, or feigning indifference?) then said: 'Well, if you must know, I'm meeting Antoine.'

I only knew of one Antoine.

'What, *the* Antoine ...'

'Yes, Mum.'

I left it at that. The conversation, clearly, wasn't for continuing. Anyway, I was already late. I needed to be at Mrs Baker's.

Driving to Kent House, directly into a low wintry sun – raising, and adjusting the car's visor at every twist and turn of the road – I found myself thinking about Antoine.

When we'd interviewed him, he'd seemed pleasant enough – tall, polite and with a scrummy French accent. From recollection, he was over here to improve his English in readiness for an MBA. But I suppose it was the timing that surprised me. We'd only interviewed him twenty-four hours earlier and presumably that's when they'd first laid eyes on each other. Quick work. There again, what with Facebook and Twitter, they probably already knew more about each other than a month's worth of dating back in my day.

But what did I know about him? Well, he certainly wasn't one of Su A's close-knit little group. In fact, from memory – I'd need to check this out – he'd come over to England on the same weekend she'd disappeared, enrolling at the school on the following Monday. So even though he qualified on my ruling (only interview students who were there when Su A was) it was on a mere technicality.

Mrs Baker's home, and Su A's home while she'd lived here, was not quite as I'd expected. I'd pictured a suburban semi, but what I found myself driving up to was a small development of modern, luxury apartments.

I parked my car in one of the two visitor spaces, walked up the neat path to the glazed front door, pressed the buzzer marked '7 – *Baker*' and was immediately greeted with a cheery 'Hello, I'll let you in' – the speed of recognition suggesting that there was a CCTV on the other side of the glass door.

The door clicked, I pushed it open and was able to confirm what I'd guessed – pointing down from the ceiling was a camera.

I walked up the carpeted stairs to where she was waiting with the front door open, smiling pleasantly. She somehow looked a little younger and perhaps less rotund than I'd remembered. Her clothes were sharper – slacks and sweater – her hair lighter and re-styled and her make-up was softer. Certainly not the Mrs Baker from a Happy Families deck.

A few little thoughts fluttered through my mind. Had she made a special effort for me, or was she always this well turned out? Then another thought. I know she was late sixties, but could she have a man in tow? Then yet another. If she has, how about back then?

Showing me in, we exchanged pleasantries without shaking hands (women greeting women often don't) but she did ask me if I wanted a cup of tea (which women of her generation always do) to which I said yes.

If Mrs Baker's flat appeared to be nice enough from the outside, it was, if anything, better still on the inside. From the spacious living room where I sat, through floor-to-ceiling picture windows, were views across Kelsey Park – with its lakes, lawns and beds – albeit now lying dormant in the winter sun. In the summer, with French windows open, sitting out on the balcony, it must have been a delight. The only other observation I made, from the furniture around me – some of which was darker, heavier and older than you would expect for such a modern flat – is that she probably had, at some stage in her life, moved from a larger house.

She came in with tea and biscuits and we sat and nattered. I call it that because it wasn't so much an interview as an almost hour-long – the time flew by – chat about anything and every-thing. Mrs Baker – 'Do call me Doris' – helped out with quite a few local organizations and belonged to a number of clubs. These ranged from going to a weekly bridge night at the golf club – she didn't play golf herself but the mention of it brought up her late husband, who had died some six years earlier – to working a couple of days in a charity shop.

Clearly, since her husband's demise, she had been getting her life back together and I would guess that taking in foreign students would have been part of that process. The company was possibly as important than the money.

It probably took over half an hour to get onto the subject of Su A. And that, precisely, was why I'd left it until the Friday – I knew this one would take time. Everything Doris Baker told me about Su A matched what everyone else had said. But when pushed she did mention that she wasn't great with directions. Apparently, when she arrived at Heathrow – admittedly after a tiring, twelve-hour flight – she'd apparently got lost between the toilets and WH Smith's. And on a couple of other occasions, whilst out and about with her friends in London, she'd got on the wrong Tube. This may not be of any great relevance, but Doris Baker had been the first person to point this out.

The big issue for me, though, was boyfriends. Ever since Eduardo, the school's receptionist, had implied in the subtlest of ways, that Chen could be more than just a friend, it had been playing on my mind. But again, I drew a blank. Yes, she went out with her friends but it was always just that – plural. On the few occasions she'd gone out with just one of them it was Yoomi. And given that Yoomi was both a fellow Korean and female, it was hardly grounds for suspicion. Oh yes, and according to her, the police had checked the flat's CCTV cameras and found nothing that suggested otherwise.

Finally, five minutes before leaving, I asked if I could check out Su A's bedroom. Doris, near to tears, stayed put.

Decent sized, with a single bed in it, Su A's bedroom had the same beautiful views of the park that the lounge did. There was nothing telling me it was a young girl's bedroom (pictures of pop stars etc.) but there again, this place was only her temporary home. Perhaps her room back in Korea conformed more to type.

There was a bedside cabinet (a few pressed hankies inside), a small wardrobe (dresses, jackets) and a chest of drawers (jumpers, cardigans).

A couple of points. Firstly, I found it mildly surprising all this stuff was still here. Then I thought about it. Of course, for Mr and Mrs Kim shipping it back to Korea would be an admittance of defeat. A sort of terrible closure. Leaving it all here would probably be what I would do.

Also, quite a lot of pink (*Hello Kitty* etc.) featured in her wardrobe, telling me pretty much what I'd have guessed. Japanese and Korean girls, even in their early twenties, often dress in a far more innocent way than their European equivalent. To Western eyes, there can be something a little unnerving about their combination of childishness and sexuality. It can also, ominously, make them all the more vulnerable to a certain type of male.

By the time it came to leaving, I felt close enough to Doris

Baker to hug her goodbye. Somehow, having just left Su A's bedroom, it seemed natural.

I left the house a sadder person but a person all the more determined to have an impact on the case.

My last meeting of the week was to be with Mr Taplow. I do realize that TV cops work twenty-four seven and that perhaps I should go on probing and digging all weekend. But I'm no TV cop. Anyway, the school, the main focus of my enquiries, closed on Friday afternoons, so the only probing and digging I'd be doing would be amongst the bargains at Primark.

This time, rather than come and collect me from reception, Taplow remained in his office, having told me to just turn up as and when I was ready. It felt better that way. The formalities were over, I knew the layout of the place better now, and it made me feel a little more like part of the team.

The first time I'd met him he'd been polite, but wary. I can't blame him for this – we'd had our differences. But I'd kept my side of the bargain – all the interviews within the school's bounds, no students taken from classes, most meetings under ten minutes in duration – and we'd now warmed to each other. I only report this point in the interests of investigative accuracy, of course. Well, obviously.

We started with a pleasant discussion about nothing in partic-ular and slowly this turned into a bit of a debriefing from me – telling him how things had gone during my first full week at his school. I was very careful not to give anything away about our threatening phone call, but was able to ask him a couple of points about pronunciation. Do really good English-speaking foreigners – those with almost no accent – sometimes say 'I am' instead of 'I'm' etc.? Apparently, yes. According to him, their English can sometimes be almost too perfect.

'For example,' he said, 'when we say *could have* we almost swallow the *have* – so much so that some people incorrectly think it's *could of* which of course it isn't. A grammatically perfect foreigner, even if he'd then lived here for a number of years, would never do this.'

Finally, we wished each other good weekends, and my week's meetings were over. Or should have been.

But what happened next changed everything.

I made my way back down the pleasantly creaky staircase (everything's nicer on a Friday) through the cheerful reception area – bidding Eduardo and Kirsty goodbye – and strolled out into the winter sunlight. Yes, it looked like being a nice weekend.

I then walked to my car, zapping the locks as I neared it, opened the door, slid in, checked my face in the mirror, clicked myself into the seatbelt and put the key in the ignition – then stopped. Under my wiper was a note. Probably put there by some over-officious bastard who didn't know I'd been given a parking slot.

I unclicked my seatbelt, opened the door, slid back out and – still only half-standing – reached across the windscreen and plucked it from the wiper. I fell back into my driving seat and, with my hands against the wheel, unfolded it.

Three lines:

저희 어머니의 성함은 박입니다.

SHE'S STILL ALIVE BUT NOT FOR LONG

THEN ANNA

ELEVEN

HEART THUMPING, THROAT dry, I scan the two lines again:

She's still alive but not for long.
Then Anna.

I scrabble for my mobile, hit contacts, scroll down, find 'Anna', punch the green button.

It rings and rings, then switches to voicemail.

Right, try to sound calm: 'Oh, Anna, it's Mum here. You, er, couldn't call back if you get the chance, could you … See you soon. Byeee.'

I hit the red button, scroll down further to 'Office' and hit green. Even before I connect, it starts to vibrate. An incoming call.

I look at the name on the screen. Thank God.

'Hi Anna.'

'Hi, Mum, sorry. I could hear it ringing but couldn't find it. It was down the side of the sofa. You all right?'

So much for sounding calm.

'Yes, fine. I was, er, just phoning to tell you I'm nearly finished.'

'Great. Erm, Mum, I was thinking of going over to my flat, if that's OK. I've got Sal with me and she's got her car. She's offered to help bring some clothes and stuff back.'

'No problem. Good idea, if Sally doesn't mind.'

'No, she's off work today anyway.'

'Give her my love, won't you.'

'Will do. See you later. Byee.'

'Bye, love.'

I hit the red, put the phone down and put my head in my hands.

Relief. Safe. And with a friend too.

Even before this, I'd been concerned about her. But now....

I took my hands from my face and looked at the note again. Whether it was from Su A's abductor or some kind of stalker didn't greatly matter. Neither sounded that appealing. *She's still alive but not for long. Then Anna.* The 'she' could refer to Anna, but more likely, it was a reference to Su A. But what that meant, surely, was that Su A is alive now, but not for much longer – then it's Anna's turn.

Leaving aside the chilling threat to Anna, and assuming the 'she' was indeed Su A, was this even possible? Could she really be, after over three months, still alive somewhere?

I turned my attention to the (presumably) Korean top line:

저희 어머니의 성함은 박입니다.

Was it just Korean for the words below it?

Then I noticed something else. Suddenly my blood ran cold.

At the beginning of the top line, just to the left of the first Korean character, was something I'd taken to be a smudge. But it wasn't a smudge. It was a fingerprint. A very deliberate fingerprint. Worse still, it was in a very suspicious rusty brown colour. Unless I was very much mistaken, it was blood.

I thought hard, reading then re-reading the whole note. Then I lifted my sights, turning my attention back to the world outside my car windows – the car park in front of me, the gates to my left, the school buildings to my right. I found myself wondering. Was he still around? Gloating?

Almost immediately, coming out of the school's main entrance, were students – one, then two, then a number. The final bell had gone. But none of them – walking down the steps, laughing, talking, gathering – looked the least bit suspicious. None of them, surely, would have done this.

I looked back down at the paper. This was a threat to Anna, yes. But it was more than that. The phone call had gone unrecorded, but this was tangible evidence. Forensic evidence too. It was also, therefore, police property. This whole thing was getting way too heavy for me.

At that point in time, sitting in my car, feeling slightly sick, slightly shivery, I simply wanted out. But whether I liked it or not, I was in. Very deep. As was Anna.

I drew breath, bit my lip, thought. What next? So far, I'd only unfolded the paper – touching it around its edges.

Carefully, very carefully, I propped the note up in front of me, between shelf and windscreen, leaned over to the passenger seat, pulled my handbag towards me and fished out my mobile. I then framed it up and took half a dozen pictures – in both landscape and portrait – of each individual line and all three lines together.

I then picked up the note by its corner, carefully re-folded it, opened the car door and placed the note back under the wind-screen wiper. Getting fully out, I took some photos of it in situ – in close up and wide. I then carefully removed the note again and put it in my bag.

I needed a translation and I was in exactly the right place. But the fewer people who knew about it, the better.

I found my way back to the busy reception, behind which, as ever, was Eduardo. Despite being mobbed by students – mostly girls – asking him about places to visit and things to see, he looked up and, almost having to shout through the crowd, asked if he could help.

'I'd like something translated, if possible.'

'From Spanish?' he asked, thinking I wanted him to do the translating.

'No, sorry – I was, er, wondering if there was a Korean student …?'

'Yes, er, Lucy, could you help Mrs Andrews, please?' he said, holding his pen up and using it to point towards me.

He was addressing a girl to my left who was with a couple of similarly Korean-looking girls. All three glanced over to me and, by simply moving back from the crowd, I was able to usher them away from the counter.

Up close, they were identikit Korean girls: doll-like faces, flawless skin, curtain-straight hair, two in bobs, one with pigtails. They also had tiny, pre-pubescent-looking bodies – despite probably being in their late teens. And the good news was that I didn't recognize any of them. I was looking for students who couldn't, under any circumstances, be connected with the case. I also didn't want them thinking I was on any kind of official business. So task number one was to put them at ease.

I started by introducing myself then asking them their names. All three of them, as is often the case, had adopted English names: Lucy, Cindy and Alice. The childlike nature of these names somehow added to their complex mixture of sexuality and innocence.

I asked them all about themselves – none had been friends before arriving, but were lifelong buddies now – and then how long they'd been here. 'Two weeks,' said Lucy. Perfect.

There were now a few vacant seats in reception, so I asked them if we could sit down – they said yes, and followed me to the chairs.

With Lucy settled to my left and Cindy and Alice to my right, I pulled my phone from my pocket and flicked through the photos until I found the clearest picture of the Korean characters.

'Here,' I said, turning the screen towards Lucy. 'Could you tell me what it says?'

I felt a little anxious. I wasn't entirely sure I should be doing this. Those words could say anything: threaten, abuse, or simply spell out someone's name. I didn't want to alarm them, but I did need answers.

Lucy thought for a second and then, holding the phone for steadiness, read out in Korean – turning it slightly towards her friends for nodding confirmation – then said: 'In English it say: "My mother's name is Park."'

'My mother's name is Park?' I checked.

'Yes.'

I thought for a second. Was this referring to Su A's mother? Logically it should be. But from memory her mother's name was SoYoung. Either way, who cares? Why the big deal?

There was no point in keeping Lucy and her friends any longer, so I thanked them and let them go.

Driving home, I thought and thought, but came up with nothing.

TWELVE

DROPPED OFF BY Sally, Anna got back just after five with a couple of bulging suitcases.

Big and bubbly, Sally was an always-there-when-you-need-her type of girl – to Anna, at least. They'd originally met at uni, where apparently they shared just about everything – even, according to Anna, boyfriends, at one stage. Not simultaneously, of course. At least, I hope not. I must say I can't quite visualize the type of boy that would suit both Anna and Sally, but he would certainly need a catholic taste in women. There again, most men do.

That was all a long time ago, of course. Now, having both established themselves in the London jobs market, they were sharing a flat too. Up until the point Anna had lost her job, that is – when she sub-let and lived with me.

Sally helped Anna upstairs with the suitcases, bounded back down, declined the offer of a cuppa, and said goodbye. Or perhaps I should say shouted it; she wasn't exactly quiet either.

I went upstairs with the ulterior motive of helping Anna put her stuff away, but she said no, she'd be fine. What I really wanted to do was find a way of telling her about the note. I'd agonized about it since leaving the school. But keeping her in blissful ignorance just wasn't an option. Apart from anything else, she had a date lined up with one of the students tonight. And even if she decided to go ahead with that, what about tomorrow night? She was now going to meet some friends Saturday too. Could I really let her wander about at night without her even knowing? Of course not. What she then did about it would be her decision, of course. But it needed to be a decision based on the facts.

So I went downstairs, made two cups of tea, took them into the living room, sat down and waited.

Eventually Anna came down the stairs, all bright and breezy – I think she was happy that another chapter of her life was neatly parcelled up. Not over – she had every intention of going back eventually – but packaged and stored, at least.

I needed to tell her pretty much immediately. I'd had some time to think about it and for two reasons time would be of the essence. Firstly, I didn't want her to start getting ready for her date before telling her. If she was going to change her plans, it was important to allow her the chance to do it with a pretence of casualness. So much of this stuff's psychological. If she was going to get through this without turning into an absolute wreck, she needed the opportunity to feign indifference – if that's what she wanted. Just as I had every intention of doing. We can't have two females freaking each other out, can we? The other reason, far more practically, was that I had a couple of bobbies coming round.

'Erm, Anna, there's something you need to know.'

'What's that, Mum?'

I held up the paper. 'That was stuck to my car.'

She looked at it, visibly whitening: 'What does it mean?'

'I'm not sure I know. The Korean words say "My mother's name is Park".'

'My mother's name is Park?'

'Yes,' I said, sipping my tea. 'I've got no idea what that's supposed to mean, but all I do know is your name is underneath it, as you can see. So I thought you should know.'

After discussing it at length, me continuing in a manner (hopefully) that was part nonchalant, part necessity, she started to follow my lead, and treat it with indifference. Probably just a crank, we agreed. But deep down, like me, she was shaken. I could tell.

Half an hour later, the police arrived, but just before that, Anna did indeed cancel her date with Antoine. Her pretext was that she could hardly be getting herself ready for a date whilst being interviewed by the police. That wasn't true. She had loads of time. But I was relieved, naturally. There'd come a time when she'd go out again, of course. There'd have to. The one thing you can't let one of these people do (I use the word 'people' loosely) is change your life. If you do, they've won. But tonight wasn't the night for brave resistance. And it certainly wasn't a night for first dates.

I was glad it was Wilkins and Pollard rather than Sullivan. One thing we didn't need was a big fat alpha male. We needed someone who would listen; someone on our side.

Firstly, of course, I made them a cup of tea. It's a strange thing, but looking back, when people visited our office, Anna always made the tea. But when someone visited our house, I seemed to. I suppose it was the switch in roles. Mum to boss, boss to mum.

The two young policemen settled straight down to business – sitting on the sofa with teas and notebooks at the ready. Wilkins, fresh-faced and boyish, was exactly the kind of copper that brings forth the old adage about policemen looking younger and younger – dark hair, brown eyes, good looks. A little earnest, maybe, but that was no bad thing. Pollard looked as his name somehow suggested: lanky, awkward and a tad dull.

I gave them the offending piece of paper, which I was alarmed to note they fingered rather more than I would have liked. By way of a heavy hint, I immediately pointed out the (probable) bloody fingerprint. This had the desired effect – Pollard lightly putting it down onto the coffee table in front of them both, well away from their teas.

I then flicked through the pictures on my mobile phone, showing them the note's position under the windscreen wiper and the car's positioning in the car park. Wilkins asked a few questions about timing etc. and Pollard diligently took notes. He then asked me if I could think of any possible culprits – anyone who could have done such a thing. I said yes, about 250. Briefly, he didn't get it. Then he smiled, realizing I was referring to the number of people at the school. OK, it was perhaps a bit face-tious, but in a way it was genuine. It could have been almost anyone. I did mention one person though. Man In (soiled) Black, Mr Paul Farrell. When asked why, I shrugged. 'No good reasons, just feminine intuition.'

Pollard suggested, smiling, that they do need slightly more than that. I reminded them, also smiling, that my suspicions on Ko Hyeon-gi – last name I'd given them – was based on just that, only to then find out that he had long-term family connections. 'So I assume you've interviewed him now,' I added mischievously.

Of course, they weren't in a position to deny or confirm this, but something told me they hadn't.

Then Wilkins asked the obvious question: had I any idea what the Korean words said?

'My mother's name is Park,' I replied.

They, like everyone else, looked confused.

'Why would he tell you that?' asked Pollard.

'I'm not sure,' I said.

'So is her mother's name really Park?' asked Pollard.

'No,' I said, 'it's SoYoung.'

'So let's get this straight …'

At that point Wilkins' phone rang, so Pollard never got to complete his question. But the confused look on his face told me everything. He, like us, was baffled.

With Wilkins on the phone and Pollard, rather annoyingly, picking up the note and fingering it further, Anna and I just sipped our teas.

What I did notice was that whoever was on the other end of the line seemed to be doing all the talking, whilst Wilkins, between increasingly long silences, was becoming more and more defensive, finally coming up with: 'But I have to deal with problems as and when they arise – whoever they are, sir.'

The penny dropped. The 'whoever' and the 'problem' was me. The 'sir' was Sullivan.

Wilkins and Pollard were getting a bollocking from Sullivan for dropping whatever they were doing and coming straight round here.

Sullivan didn't like me, less so since my involvement in this case. But this was unfair. What wasn't urgent now? What wasn't important? OK, I could just about see why they hadn't got round to interviewing Hyeon-gi yet. What's another interview in a three-month-old case? But this was no longer a three-month-old case. It was alive and kicking – as was Su A, if the forensic evidence turned out as I expected.

What I'd like to have done is ask Wilkins if I could speak to Sullivan. Make my point there and then. But that wouldn't have helped anything or anyone. Look bad for Pollard and Wilkins, and achieve nothing for us.

So I just pretended I didn't know what was going on, and let it come to a natural end – assuming anything to do with Sullivan comes to a natural end.

Once he'd finished, putting his phone away and looking a shade paler, I offered them both another tea. But they declined and left.

The whole interview had taken perhaps twenty minutes, of which a good ten had been taken up by Sullivan's unnecessary interference. I was furious, but kept it to myself. The last thing Anna needed was me ranting on about my old boss. It would give her the feeling that the police weren't taking the case seriously. Which, of course, they weren't.

So I just let it drop and seethed. I would speak to Sullivan, sooner rather than later, but not within earshot of Anna.

I decided to take a shower; felt as though the grime needed washing away, the hot, steamy water drawing out all the fear and the filth of the day. Afterwards, I spent some time sprucing myself up – new make-up, new jeans and favourite sweater. I was consciously avoiding the trap of just slopping around in a dressing gown. That might have sent out the wrong message to Anna. From experience, I know that the stalked and the hounded, the bullied and the beaten, can just fold in on themselves. When I say from experience, by the way, I mean police experience, not personal experience. No one ever bullied me into submission.

When I went downstairs, Anna was immediately complimentary: 'You look nice – off anywhere?'

It worked. OK, it's only a tiny thing, but it brightened her up a little and, more importantly, made her think I might, just, be going out somewhere. Of course, I had absolutely no intention of leaving her that night, but by letting her think it was a possibility and by casually answering, 'No, but I need to pop to the shops before they close,' I gave her the impression that her situation didn't faze me – which in truth, it did.

'Erm, Mum,' she said, 'before you go … I've been thinking about that note.'

I was sure she had; so had I. It was pretty much all I'd been thinking about.

'Oh, yeah,' I answered, offhandedly.

'Well, you know it said my mother's name is such and such?'

'Yes.'

'Maybe it means her second name.'

I had already considered this, but it didn't seem likely. Frankly, it didn't add much. Even if her full name was So Young *Park* Kim, so what?

'So you mean, like … her middle name?' I said, doubtfully.

'No, no – her *original* name – her *maiden* name: *"My mother's maiden name is …"'*

I thought for a second: *'My mother's maiden name is Park'*, *'My mother's maiden name is Park.'*

'Brilliant!' I said.

She was right. What's the question you get asked when you need to prove who you are – from banks etc? What's the question you answer when you've forgotten a password? It's the name nobody else knows. Your mother's maiden name!

I immediately found my bag, fished out the phone, switched it on and found the photo of the note. If I used Anna's translation it now read:

'My mother's maiden name is Park' (written by the victim, under duress, proving who she is).

'She's still alive but not for long' (written by abductor, stating the chillingly obvious).

'Then Anna' (written by abductor, stating the chillingly obvious).

I sat down on the sofa, silently, eyes fixed to the image. Then Anna sat down next to me. After a while I said: 'You know, Anna, if this maiden name thing has been slightly lost in translation, which it sounds like it has, it could tell us a lot.'

'How do you mean?'

'Well, firstly, the person holding her must have some knowledge of Korean. Otherwise Su A – assuming it is Su A – could have written anything. I mean, think about it, he asks her to write such and such and she writes: *"I'm being held at 35 Acacia Avenue, Bromley by Mr Joe Bloggs."'*

Anna smiled at this. It was ridiculous, but true. But then she shrugged and said: 'But he could've translated it – you know, on the internet– then got her to copy it out.'

'True, but would you really trust that?' I turned the characters towards her. 'I mean, look at those dots and squiggles. Unless you read Korean, could you honestly be sure she wasn't adding some hidden clue as to where she's being held? No. Unless he can translate, *and she knows* he can translate – that's crucial too – he's asking for trouble.'

Anna said nothing, but clearly agreed. That was important to me. I valued her judgement.

'Now this guy's not stupid, and he knows we're not stupid either. He knows *we* know he's not stupid. Therefore he's either actually Korean or wants us to believe he is. Now assuming we're right about this thumbprint – and obviously the police will check this out – Su A's been forced to put it there, right?'

Anna nodded.

'And she's been forced to write the Korean characters too. Now, think about it. We got this translated by three Korean girls and not one of them mentioned anything about maiden names. They translated exactly what they saw. Either they're wrong, the writer's wrong, or we're guessing wrong. And I don't think we are. We need to speak to a Korean speaker. Find out what Su A was trying to say – or being forced to say – and why it differs from what's actually on there.'

THIRTEEN

LATE NOVEMBER, EARLY darkness, faint smell of bonfires in the air. I didn't need to pop to the shops at all – just get out of the house. Show Anna I was happy to leave her alone, that some creepy little saddo couldn't turn us into victims. Mostly, though, to make a phone call. A phone call I didn't want her to hear.

As I left the house, the security light flicked on and, by the time I reached the gate, flicked off again. Funny, the dozen seconds it remained on had always seemed long enough. Suddenly it wasn't. I must re-set it.

My thick coat, hurriedly thrown across my shoulders, failed to stop me shivering. The front gate, only partially lit by orange street lights, creaked open, and my footsteps echoed on the wet paving.

I didn't walk far. Didn't need to.

No unsolicited notes on my windscreen. I zapped the locks, the interior light came on (ridiculous, I know, but I was relieved to find no one sitting inside) and I got in. The light faded off. Back in darkness. I centrally locked the car from the inside – something I'd never normally do.

Originally, I had the idea of driving for a bit – perhaps two or three minutes – before parking up and then making my phone call. Again, just to make a point, to show Anna that we could. But once inside, I changed my mind. From where I sat I could see the house. Anna wouldn't know I hadn't moved – the curtains hadn't flicked – so I decided to stay put.

I grappled the interior light above me, switching it back on, then took my mobile out from my bag, pressed contacts – the screen light further illuminating the car – scrolled down to 'w' (I still had police filed under 'work') and dialled. He wouldn't take my call, so I'd devised a plan.

A few years ago Sullivan had had a fling with a WPC about a dozen years his junior. Everyone knew it – except his wife, that is. Later, when the whole thing started getting messy, she asked for a transfer and got it. Sullivan's accommodating like that. The WPC's name was Pat Simeon. Now if there was one call he'd take it would be from her. Who knows, she might be up for a bit of old-flame rekindling. Or possibly phoning to threaten him – finally spill the beans. Either way, he'd take it. He'd have to.

'Hello, can I speak to David Sullivan please?'

'Who can I say is calling?'

'It's Pat Simeon.'

There was a brief silence while I waited to be transferred.

Suddenly, Sullivan's voice – far softer and friendlier-sounding than anything I'd ever been on the receiving end of. 'Hello, Patsy! Long time, no see!'

'Patsy?' I said. 'Who said anything about Patsy? This is Pamela, Pamela Andrews.'

Another silence. Silences are supposed to be golden. This one was leaden.

'Oh, er, how are you?' he finally said.

'Not good, frankly.'

'Oh, and why's that?'

'Well, problem number one is that I've got this nasty little stalker threatening my daughter. And problem number two is that the police don't seem to be that bothered.'

'Oh, really, and why do you say that?'

'Because the two very nice bobbies who came round this afternoon got a right bollocking from their boss – within earshot of me – which apart from anything is unprofessional.'

'I'm not sure what you're referring to, but perhaps they had other work to do – the world doesn't revolve around you,

Pamela – *and* I don't think you should be listening in on other people's private calls.'

'Listening in! I could hear your voice the other side of the bloody room!'

'Look,' he said, 'your case will be dealt with in due course – like the many others we're dealing with.'

I took a breath, calmed down, continued: 'OK, then why haven't you even interviewed the name I gave you?'

'Who we do and don't interview is our business. You're no longer in the force, remember?'

'David?' I asked, politely.

'Yes, Pamela,' he replied, even more politely

'Have you seen this stuff?'

'What stuff?'

'The stuff I gave Wilkins.'

'Not yet, no. Like I said, we've got plenty of other –'

'I do realize how busy you are. I used to work with you, remember? But I really think you should check it out. Apart from anything else, it proves that Su A is still alive.'

All I got down the phone was yet another silence. The enormity of that statement, even from me – someone he didn't like or trust – was temporarily dumbfounding.

'Did you hear me, David? She's still alive.'

'How do you know?'

'Just look at it – and while you're at it, get forensics to check the bloody thumbprint too. And David, when I say bloody thumbprint, I'm referring to a thumbprint *made* of blood.'

There was no response to this either. He probably didn't even know about the thumbprint made of blood.

'Look, David, so far I've played this your way, co-operated in every way. Names, dates, evidence – verbal and written – I've handed you the lot ...'

'As you're duty-bound to.'

'Yes, as I'm duty-bound to – and so far I've told the papers nothing. Now if I was just a glory hunter – as you seem to think

– I wouldn't have played it that way, would I? I'd be all over the front pages by now. But if you want that, fine. How would *"Mum and Daughter Team: Su Still Alive!"* sound over your morning cornflakes, David?'

Sullivan collected his thoughts. 'Look, as ever, I'll do what's best for her. Now if you'll let me get on with my work …'

'All I'm asking for is a bit of protection. I'm not expecting twenty-four-hour surveillance, just the occasional panda car going past my window. Alternatively, as I said, we can go the other route. Just think on, David, just think on.'

With that, I rang off.

I can't say I noticed any great police presence that weekend. Mind you, we didn't get out of the house much, despite the clear, wintry weather. For reasons unspoken, yet mutually understood, we stayed in – long lie-ins, late breakfasts, Anna slumbering on the sofa, me pottering in the garden. Yet, despite seeing neither hair nor hide of any police presence, I knew my rant at Sullivan would have hit the mark. He wasn't stupid. He would cover his arse, at the least. His itinerary would probably go something like: 1) contact Wilkins and Pollard 2) look at evidence 3) realize its magnitude 4) give opposite bollocking: *'Why the fuck didn't you show it to me sooner?'* 5) knock up a few diktats about 'all singing from the same song sheet' etc. 6) go home 7) kick the wife. He'd also know he'd need to up his game a bit – or be shown to be. If something untoward had happened to either Su A or Anna, he'd be in serious trouble.

One interesting thing did happen, though. I was in the garden cutting back shrubs and clearing up leaves – Saturday was fine and cold – when Anna came to the French windows, still in dressing gown, and shouted, 'Mu-*um*, pho-*own*.' Incidentally, whenever anyone called, it was 'Mu-*um*, pho-*own*'. Like I didn't know what that black plastic object in her hand was called. Anyway, with dirty hands and dishevelled hair, I took the call.

Edward Taplow. And he wasn't ringing about the school, and

wasn't ringing about Su A. Once past his stuttering opening, it became apparent. A date, bless him!

He sounded as though he'd been rehearsing and rehearsing his little speech since our last meeting – probably wanted to bring it up then – which I thought was quite sweet.

Was I flattered? You bet. Tall, fit and, in a scholarly way, handsome. And at my age, it wasn't every day that handsome men came a-knocking.

So did I say yes? No, I'm afraid I didn't. As ever, Anna came first. There was no way I was leaving her home alone. Actually, once I'd put the phone back, once I was back in the garden digging up a particularly stubborn weed, I thought further about it and was even more certain I had made the right decision. After all, in my book, Edward Taplow wasn't in the clear – no one at that school was. What better way to get me out of the way than to ask me to some restaurant, leaving Anna alone in the house? Over-suspicious? Maybe. But as I've told you many times, I'm two things: detective *and* mum. And in this case the roles overlapped.

Maybe it was something in the air that weekend, but I believe Anna had a phone call too – which I took to be Antoine. I'm only assuming this, though. I suppose it could have been anyone.

I hadn't heard the phone go – no chance of me reciprocating with 'An-*na*, pho-*own*' – so she must have done the dialling. I'd gone upstairs, run a hot bath and blissfully soaked away the gardening grime, then redressed. It was only sixish and I was looking forward to cracking open the Pinot. Coming down the stairs, I caught sight of her, hand cupped over phone, talking in hushed tones.

I didn't ask her who it was, of course. Wanted to, but didn't. If it were Antoine, I'd like to think that she was a little circumspect, keep things sketchy on the cancelled date front – blame a heavy workload, or something. She's a sensible enough girl so I was sure she'd be careful. And if she was setting up another date, fair enough. She could hardly stay at home for ever, could she?

FOURTEEN

MONDAY. DECEMBER THE first. The bright, clear weather was never going to last. And it didn't. Bucketing down. Cascading from roofs, overflowing from gutters, gushing from downpipes.

Anna, me, standing in porch. Umbrellas up: *'Run!'*

House to car, splashing, screaming like kids, reach car, fumble for keys – still holding umbrella, zap door, scramble in, closing door while collapsing umbrella – not possible – drenched anyway. Doors slammed. Exhaling and elated, laughing like children.

Windows steamed up, rain pounding roof. Switch on car, can't even hear engine, can't even hear radio. Demister on – no impression. Wipers on – ditto. Like a waterfall. *'Phew.'* Demister to max. Wipers to max. Wait to clear.

Coats damp and wool-smelling. Anna still breathless. I hate wipers at maximum. I feel as if I have to do everything double quick.

Clearing now – the windows, not the weather – I look in mirror, indicate, edge out. Through gears carefully, wipers racing, but not coping. Cars are slowing down. Aquaplaning – roads like rivers. We edge past a gurgling spout of water – an overwhelmed drain – to the bottom of the hill. A newly formed lake. Carefully, slowly fording it, almost cringing behind the wheel. We reach the other side – to relative sanctuary. Absurd, yet exhilarating. What a way to start a week.

*

Funny, the way you picture things. I'd imagined parking near the spot where the note had been attached, only this time with Anna. What would I say? Would I walk around the car pointing it all out? After all, we were supposed to be detectives. Or would I say nothing? Well, as it happened, none of that was relevant. The ridiculous rain changed everything.

I pulled up to the school's front steps – Anna clambering out, attempting the reverse door/umbrella routine. Just as impossible, just as soaking.

I drove on, parked up, re-umbrellered and ran. Across flooded car park, up steps, reached hallway – drenched again. Laughing again.

The other event I'd vaguely pictured was meeting up with Edward Taplow. Would it be awkward? Would he say something? Should I?

I suppose being a Monday had something to do with these ruminations. I frequently suffer mild paranoia about the week ahead – often about things which really aren't that important. Mondays magnify. Well, anyway, I needn't have worried. The meeting Taplow problem was wiped out by the weather too. He was already in the hallway speaking to Anna: she dripping everywhere, he wryly amused, or maybe dryly amused. In a very British way, conversations were now revolving around the weather – no other subjects worthy of discussion. So after a few sarcastic remarks about probable water shortages later in the year, we moved off – he to the staff room, we dripping our way to our little cubby hole.

It takes a while to get organized when you're wet. At least, it does for me. Brollies, macs, hair and coffee requirements – procured by Anna, in this case.

As it turned out, I was pleased I'd got her involved in the whole interview process the week before. Had I not, my real reason for leaving her alone would have been obvious. But because we'd already conducted interviews together, I could maintain it was necessary.

We soon settled back into a rhythm – me behind the small table, facing the door, Anna to my right, as out-facing as possible (which it wasn't very), interviewees squeezing in between open door and table.

I got the distinct impression the students loved it. In fact, I was told, rather ruefully by Christine, one of the office staff, that miraculously, no student had ever been absent on their interview day. 'Perhaps you should be a permanent fixture,' she'd joked.

There were two issues, on the maiden name issue, I needed to clear up quickly. First: was the note actually saying that? After all, it's not what the Korean girls had said. And second: was Su A's mother's pre-marital name actually Park?

Now I could have checked this out in a number of ways – all of which I'd considered. I could have rung up Ko Hyeon-gi – that's what he was there for, both as a translator and a friend of the family. I'd get an instant answer, but would I trust it? Next option would be to email the Kims. But their English was poor. After all, if the term 'maiden name' was being lost in translation, what chance did I have on an email? More importantly, though, telling them about notes on my windscreen might give them false hope *and* scare the life out of them. So I'd decided to wait until today, when Yoomi Lee, one of Su A's best friends, was available for an interview.

At nineteen years of age, Yoomi was five years younger than Su A and probably, had they not been thrown together on this cold, alien little island, would never have become best friends – five years at that age being quite an age gap. But become friends, apparently, they had – meeting up after school, going shopping and sharing all the things young girls share. And that made this interview vital. I had a million questions to ask.

The most noticeable difference between them – something that was apparent from the photos I'd seen of them together – was height. Whereas Su A was short and perhaps a little dumpy, Yoomi was tall and willowy, particularly for a Korean. She was one of those girls that probably didn't attract too much attention from the boys yet – small boobs and large tooth-brace – but with her slender body and high cheek-bones would probably blossom into the more classically beautiful.

She was wearing ultra-flat ballet-like shoes, jeans so clingy they were almost stockings and, in complete contrast, a sloppy, pink sweater. If I were to play the psychologist, I would say the bottom half was there to show off her slimness and the top half to hide her lack of bust. There again I'm not, so it could all just be down to fashion.

Her handshake was so soft it hardly existed – I somehow imagined a curtsy being more suitable – and when she sat down, despite her height, she seemed one of the few interviewees to not crowd that tiny table.

Covertly, I watched Anna watching her and could almost read my daughter's mind. Stunning, she was thinking – and she was – yet slightly weird. That's it! That's where I'd seen a being like this before: through 3D spectacles at the cinema. One of those big-eyed beauties out of *Avatar*.

She'd been away taking her IELTS exams, so I asked her how they'd gone. 'No good,' she answered. So I asked her why and, using pidgin English, she explained that the speaking part of her test had been 'terrible bad'. It hardly needed stating.

I wanted to give Yoomi more time than I'd given the other interviewees because, quite simply, she deserved it. OK, her loss was not a parent's loss, or perhaps a host parent's loss. But it was a friend's loss. And friendships at that age are for life – even if, in reality, they seldom are. The other reason I wanted to invest time in this interview was because more than most, it called for it. I had an awful lot of questions for Yoomi.

By and large, despite the broken English, I got the same old answers back about Su A: a quiet girl who wouldn't dream of going off anywhere alone.

According to Yoomi – and the school's records backed this up

– during the week prior to her disappearance, Su A had been in every class, eaten her lunches in the student canteen, and attended all three lectures, the two lectureless evenings being filled with homework.

Therefore, everything pointed towards her disappearance being simply a case of wrong place, wrong time – just some random chancer snatching her off the street. Except for one thing, or perhaps two. The phone call and the note. They weren't the work of a chancer. They pointed the other way – to the school.

So was there one occasion, at least, when she did do a bit of partying, did perhaps mix socially with teachers, staff and students? Well, according to Paul Farrell, lecturer and teacher, there was. So I asked Yoomi for confirmation. Was it true that after his lecture on Myths and Magic, they'd all gone down to the George?

'Yes,' she confirmed. 'We went George.'

'Who's we?' I asked.

She pointed to herself, said 'I', and then added: 'Carlos, Victor … Nadija … Arman.'

I noticed Anna flipping back through her notes. Like me, she was probably thinking there was at least one name missing. Anna then mouthed the word 'Chen' to me.

'Ah yes,' I said. 'What about Chen?'

'Yes,' she said.

I found this exasperating. OK, she now admitted Chen was also there – and had finally come up with all the names we'd expected – but hadn't acknowledged her original error. Was she being evasive or did she just not understand? Even her face gave nothing away – so expressionless (if beautiful) that I simply couldn't read it.

'So you, Su A, Carlos, Victor, Nadija, Arman and Chen?'

'Yes,' she confirmed.

'OK,' I said. 'Could you tell me if any of these were special friends – you know, *really* special friends?'

Blank. Nothing.

'Let me put it another way. Did she have … did Su A have a boyfriend?'

'No boyfriend,' she said quickly. (Too quickly?)

'Yoomi?' I asked, looking straight at her.

'Yes?'

'Was Chen her boyfriend?'

'No boyfriend,' she repeated – again, almost immediately.

'But he was a good friend?'

She just stuck out her lip a little. If he was, she didn't seem to think so. Or simply wasn't saying.

'Could you tell me something then, Yoomi?'

She just looked at me blankly.

'Could you tell me why, if you are her best friend, and Chen is *not* her boyfriend, she called him first – when she was in trouble, I mean?'

'Chen not boyfriend,' she simply repeated.

I clearly wasn't going to get anywhere with this, but I still had my suspicions – more so, if anything. Oh well, let's just move on. Chen was going to be one of my next interviews. I could put it to him straight.

'OK, so you've told us about her friends that night, but how about other people?'

'Other?'

'You know, other students, teachers. Who else was there?'

'Many students.'

'What about staff? Teachers, for example.'

She thought for a second, then said, 'Lecturer, he there.'

'At the pub?'

'Yes, lecturer there.'

I looked at Anna, and Anna looked at me. This was a complete contradiction of what Farrell had told us. Anna then started thumbing back through her notes, while I pushed her further.

'You mean Paul Farrell – at the pub?'

'Yes. Mr Farrell, he there.'
'You're absolutely sure?'
'Yes, he there.'

FIFTEEN

THE INTERVIEW WITH Yoomi, partly due to her poor English, partly because I had so much to ask her, was turning out to be the longest to date. But extracting information from her about the likes of Chen Choi and Farrell wasn't the sole reason for speaking to her. After all, even if her English was poor, her Korean wasn't. So with her still sitting there impassively – probably fed up with the whole thing by now – I took out my mobile, pulled up a photo of the note, leaned across the table and turned it towards her.

'Could you tell me what this says, Yoomi?'

Without pause she said, *'My mother. Her name Park.'*

Pretty much identical, the slight grammatical difference apart.

'And is that true?'

'True?'

'Is Su A's mother's name Park? I mean her original family name?'

'Yes.'

'So Park is her maiden name?'

'Maiden name?'

'Yes, maiden name. You know, the name she had before she got married.'

'No … Yes … Name now.'

This was getting more and more confusing. We were getting yes and no in the same bloody answer.

It took Anna, holding up her finger, to come to my rescue:

'Erm, Yoomi, are you saying women in Korea keep their same name – not like in England?'

She thought for a second, clearly translating Anna's words in her head. 'Yes,' she finally said. 'Korean woman keep name.'

At last we had our answer. Park was her mother's married name *and* her family name – Korean brides simply don't change their name.

Once this penny had dropped, we clarified it all one last time, asked her a couple more minor questions, thanked her kindly and allowed her to go – commiserating with her at the loss of her friend, and promising to do everything in our power to get her back, as we ushered her to the door. Whether she understood all this, or indeed half of what we'd been saying, was open to question.

Back at the table, we exhaled and debriefed. 'Well done,' I said. 'You've cracked it.'

'Not really,' said Anna, 'I mean, we pretty much knew who the note was about – now we've just got it confirmed.'

'Not that,' I said. 'The big step forward is the Korean women thing. And getting that out of her was down to you.'

'I don't see why that's so important.' She shrugged.

'It tells us loads. It tells us the person who's holding her isn't Korean, for a start. It might be the classic security checker over here – *My mother's maiden name is blah, blah* – but it just wouldn't apply in Korea. Any Korean would know that it doesn't prove anything. But the person holding her didn't know that. He simply thought up the most obvious proof of identity he could – forced her to write it down.'

Anna thought for a while, nodding a little, then frowned and said: 'But I still don't really see the need for it. After all, he put her fingerprint on it. Why bother?'

'Belt and braces,' I replied. 'Anyway, possibly the thumbprint was an afterthought – the note was the original idea. And even if it wasn't, even if he'd always planned the thumbprint, he'd still need to put it on something, wouldn't he? After all, if it'd been blank, if it'd been just a small fingerprint on a piece of blank paper, I might have thrown it away. So why not have a piece of paper with a message on it – from Su A and in Korean? It makes sense.'

I then thought for a second. 'Ironic, really. He thought he was being clever, providing proof of who she was. But the only proof he's provided is who *he* is – well, partly.'

'OK,' said Anna, leaning back. 'So who is he?'

'Well,' I said. 'I don't know exactly, but remember what I said about him needing to be able to read the note otherwise she could've been giving him away?'

Anna just nodded.

'Well, that tells us he understands Korean – or *some* Korean. Now we know he almost certainly *isn't* Korean – he's made a big blunder.'

'Right,' said Anna, taking a sip of coffee. 'And seeing as the note was put on the car here –' She gestured outward '– he's probably local, possibly from the school.'

'Exactly,' I said, ticking off the points on my finger. 'Not Korean, but speaks it. From the school, or near it. Not a bad morning's work.'

Taking a breather from our cramped little room, walking through the school's main hall, we bumped into PCs Wilkins and Pollard. Absolutely drenched.

'Morning,' I said to them brightly. 'Nice day.'

'Morning,' replied Wilkins, droplets of rain falling from his nose. 'You couldn't tell me where I'd find Mr Taplow's office, could you?'

'Yes, up the stairs on the right. But you might want to call into reception first,' I said, pointing to the sign right behind him.

'Ah, right,' he said. 'Thanks.'

Off they wandered, watering the wooden floor as they went.

They clearly hadn't come to see us, but to interview, or possibly re-interview, pupils and staff. They'd been checking out the car park, thus the drenching. Good. Not so much for the soaking – though I did find that amusing – but for at least showing their faces.

There was perhaps one tiny downside, though. I did find myself wishing they'd kicked off their enquiries – or perhaps re-enquiries – somewhere else. I could well imagine the school getting hacked off with all this. Two groups interviewing the same staff and pupils was one group too many.

'Oh, Jamie,' I said, as they made for reception (I must admit, I did rather like addressing police officers by their first name), 'Su A's mother is definitely called So Young Park.'

'Yes', he said. 'We know.'

'Good,' I added. 'And perhaps you also know that they don't have maiden names in Korea.'

'They don't?' said Pollard.

Wilkins immediately shot a wince in the direction of his colleague. It was obviously OK finding stuff out from me, but less so admitting you needed to.

'Um, thanks,' said Wilkins dolefully, as Pollard pulled out a notebook from his wet uniform to jot down this information.

I did feel a little sorry for them. I knew what it was like working for Sullivan. Still, at least they had one more piece of the jigsaw. Whether they could piece it together, as Anna and I had, was up to them. Wilkins and Pollard were very likeable lads, and there would be others working on this in the background, but I was hoping for someone a little more heavyweight at the coal face, so to speak. On the other hand, I wouldn't want the likes of Sullivan stomping around the place either.

We got ourselves a plastic cup of water from the water cooler in the now-empty staff room – I was very conscious of being in everyone's way, which was why I'd waited until the lessons started – and made our way back to our little room.

Just as we sat down, and our next interviewee, caretaker John Church, was popping his head round the door, my mobile rang. 'Oh, sorry,' I said to Church, 'do take a seat.'

The call was from Ko Hyeon-gi. I took it, but immediately regretted it.

'What the fuck do you think you're doing?'

'Erm, sorry, Ko, could I ring you—'

'No, you bloody can't! You have got no right to point fingers at me!'

'Point ... pardon?'

'Don't act the innocent with me. You put the police on to me ...'

'I gave the police some names – that's my job.'

As he yelled something about me working for him, not vice versa, Anna had the good sense to apologize to the caretaker and quickly escort him back out of the room. The conversation was clearly becoming audible.

'Look,' I said, settling back a little and now able to respond, 'my job is to find Su A – by whatever legal means I can. Frankly, if the police wanted to interview me, or Anna or whoever, I would be more than willing.'

'Interview? Who said anything about interview? They have turned my fucking place over.'

I must admit this shocked me. They were clearly now taking this case very seriously indeed. 'Look, Ko, what the police do or don't do is up to them. Take it up with them.'

'Oh, I will, I will. But in the meantime, you're fired. You're not getting another penny out of me.'

'OK, but do Su A's parents know this?'

'That's my business. I chose you, I pay you.'

'Yes, with *their* money. Tell you what, Ko, I'll just send them an email explaining what's happening, shall I? Tell them the police suspect you and that's why I'm off the case. That'll look good, won't it?'

I got no response to this so I just ploughed on: 'And if the police do take any action, how would sacking me look? That would look good for you, wouldn't it?'

'If the police do take action? What are you bloody implying?'

'Look, Ko, I'm an ex-copper, I know how these things work. The only way they could search your house is if there's something else. Me just putting your name on a list isn't enough.'

'So you're saying …'

'I'm saying there must be something. In the past, maybe. You know what it is, they know what it is, but I don't – and nor, presumably, do Mr and Mrs Kim. Let's keep it that way.'

All I could hear down the line was breathing. He was furious, but beaten.

'Think about it, Ko. The worst thing you could do is sack me. Anyway, it wouldn't stop me now – I'm in far too deep already.'

And I was.

SIXTEEN

SCHOOL CARETAKERS, DUE to a couple of high-profile cases, seem to be prime suspects. Yet in my thirty-odd years in the force I can't recall hauling in a single caretaker for anything – least of all abduction or murder. Anyway, in this case, he certainly wasn't a suspect – he had a rock-solid alibi.

John Church – Churchy to most – was about forty-five years old, squat-bodied, Velcro-headed and permanently overalled. He also had a gold earring in one ear, a chewed pencil behind the other, and a nicotine-stained right hand from roll-ups. I'd seen him standing in the yard, weighing up some task or other, slowly a-rolling and a-licking.

Churchy's alibi was a football match. I knew this from an earlier interview with one of the lecturers. Not Paul Farrell, the Myths and Magic man, but the other lecturer – Albert Christopher, Mr Ancient Britain.

Albert had told me – boring me senseless with his twin hobbies of Saxons and Druids, and Charlton Athletic Football Club – that a group of them, including Churchy, had travelled to Plymouth that weekend for an away match. So the caretaker, in this case, was in the clear – as, of course, was Christopher.

But I was no longer solely interested in what people were doing three months ago, but three days ago – the day the note appeared on my windscreen – and he, more than anybody, was the eyes and ears of the school and its grounds.

'You didn't notice anything out of the ordinary last Friday, I suppose?'

'You too!' he replied.

'Why?' I asked. 'Has someone else been asking?'

'The Old Bill,' he said. 'They've been asking everyone. Even took the CCTV tapes away.'

I was pleased to hear it. I only wished I had access to them too. I asked him what areas the cameras covered and he said, as I'd guessed, only the front entrance. I also asked him if he'd noticed anything suspicious that day, particularly around the car park, and he said no.

For his part, he asked me what happened that was such a big deal and I told him I couldn't really give him that information. 'Must've been important, that's all I can say,' he replied. 'There's more Old Bill about now than there was when that poor girl disappeared in the first place.'

That comment made me, and presumably Anna, feel a whole lot happier. It was a major achievement on the finding Su A front too.

The delay in interviewing Churchy had a knock-on effect on the next couple of interviews and we ended up contacting reception to reschedule our meeting with Chen Choi – it would have to wait until after lunch.

This allowed us a slightly earlier break, making firstly for the ladies (from bitter, leg-crossing experience we'd learned to get in before the lesson bell went), then for the canteen. But walking down the corridors we were, so to speak, beaten by the bell and by the time we got to the canteen queues were forming and tables were filling, so we decided to change tack and eat out.

We made our way back down the corridors to the main hall and, peering doubtfully out of the main windows, decided that the weather had improved sufficiently – just – to leave the building and find a local café.

Still dingy enough for cars to have their lights on, still damp enough for me to use an umbrella (though not Anna – my hair tended to frizz, whereas hers didn't), it only took us five minutes to walk to the Kent House Deli. Once inside, I ordered the food – tuna melt and latte for me, panini and cappuccino for Anna – whilst she quickly bagged a table. We were only minutes ahead of the students. They would soon be swamping this place too.

She asked me how I thought the case was going – *really* going – from the police's perspective. Interesting question. I shrugged and said that though they wouldn't exactly be delighted – the police never are –they'd definitely feel they were getting there.

'And do you think so?' she asked.

'Yes, I do,' I said. 'I mean, I don't think it's Hyeon-gi, despite what the police may think. He wouldn't have made that maiden name mistake. But whoever it is, whether they get him now, or in some cold-case review, one way or another, they'll eventually get him.'

'So where does that leave us?'

'Helping them,' I said, stating the obvious.

'But they don't want our help, do they?'

'No, but ...'

I began to get an inkling of where this was going, but I didn't say as much.

'You know Hyeon-gi wants us off the case?' she said.

'Yes.' I nodded – I could hardly disagree. My ears were still burning from his call.

Anna paused, thought, and then said: 'And the police too.'

Again, I nodded.

'Well, I don't want you to take this the wrong way, Mum, but ...'

I noticed that she was fiddling with the napkin, winding it round and round her finger.

'If everyone wants us off it, why are we still on it?'

I thought for a second. It was a very good question.

'Well,' I said, 'because Su A's parents want us on it.'

'How do you know? I mean, they're in Korea.'

OK. Now I was certain as to where it was going.

'Do you want us to drop this, Anna?'

'No … No, Mum. If you think we … you … should carry on, then …'

'But you want out, don't you?'

'It's not like that, it's….' She thought for a moment, considering her next words: 'You see, I suppose I sort of want my life back.'

I said nothing, just let her continue.

'I mean, this can't go on, can it?'

I'm not sure I understood what she meant. 'What can't go on?'

'I'm spending every minute of every day with you. I don't go out anywhere. It's not healthy, Mum – plus the fact that I'll need to go to London to do some interviews soon. How am I going to do that?'

Now I understood. The unsaid stuff – the stuff neither of us were admitting to. We'd both been pretending it was making no difference to our lives. But that's exactly what it was doing. And, as she said, she simply wanted her life back.

What I could have said to her, perhaps should have said to her, was that it was too late for all that. That it probably wouldn't make any difference now. He had sought us out, he had targeted us; not vice versa. In fact, if we threw in the towel now, it could give him even more confidence. But of course I didn't say any of that. If she wanted us to quit, we'd quit – I was feeling guilty enough about the whole situation already.

'I don't mean now, Mum,' she said. 'I don't mean this minute. It's just that, well, if we're not wanted … I mean …'

And we kind of left it at that. I fully understood, of course. I'd do what she wanted. So I just said yes, she was right, we should quit.

Walking back from the café, weather slightly better, brolly now down and talking about other things, I decided on the timeframe. We'd finish today's interviews then call it a day. In many ways, it did make sense. Apart from Chen – the boy who took the so-called 'fortune teller' call – I'd now interviewed everybody I really wanted to. And I was due to interview him next, so by the end of the day it would be job done on the interview front at least. There were other members of her little group that I hadn't spoken to – Nadija, Arman, Viktor and Carlos – but they'd all gone home long ago. So unless Hyeon-gi was going to up our expenses and jet us off to interview ex-students in faraway places, it was never going to be an option. And anyway, we now had proof that the perpetrator was still in the area, so why go traipsing around the world?

So in many ways Anna was right. It was job done, pretty much. After all, we'd been hired as Cheryl Cole and her mum, not Mrs Márple and her daughter.

Quitting was only half the problem, though. He, whoever he was, also needed to know we were quitting. Otherwise, what would be the point?

Once back at my little desk, in the minutes before Anna rejoined me – she was in the loo – I found myself thinking about our options. I could hardly put a sign on the front door saying *'Dear Mr or Mrs Abductor, Anna & Pam are now officially off the Su A case'*, could I? I couldn't really tell the press either. After all, I'd have to tell them *why* we were quitting. Just throwing in the towel wouldn't be newsworthy enough – and if it didn't make the news, how would whoever-he-is know? On the other hand, telling the press *why* would mean disclosing police evidence before it was released. And anyway, I didn't want the whole world knowing about Anna's situation.

So in the end, I decided that the best thing would be to tell Taplow, who in turn would tell his staff. The reason we were quitting would be simple – the police are back on the case, so our job is done. Then, if I was guessing right, the news would filter through. I was pretty certain, one way or another, that he or she was still connected to the school.

When Anna came back I told her – made it sound positive. She was right, it did all make sense. She just sipped water, didn't say much and listened. Perhaps she felt guilty. But if she did, she shouldn't have. She was absolutely right.

I suggested that we start by telling Edward Taplow that very afternoon – thanking him and his staff for their co-operation, and for the use of this little room. She said it didn't have to be that quick – that we could carry on till the end of the week. I said I couldn't see the point. And yet again, for the umpteenth time, I said she was right. And she was.

So that just left one interview. Mr 'Mudang', Mr 'Fortune Teller', Mr Chen Choi.

SEVENTEEN

I'D SEEN CHEN Choi from a distance, but never up close. So I already knew he was tallish – for a Korean – and already knew he was slim and already knew he was twenty-four years old. On this occasion, and in fact on the other couple of occasions I'd seen him, he was wearing low-slung drainpipes and an equally close-fitting bum-freezer jacket. Whether those outfits had been coupled with a white, penny-round shirt and a parallel, black leather tie – early Beatles-esque – I couldn't say because he'd been too far away, but they certainly were this time.

It had struck me before just how incongruous some of these Korean and Japanese students must look in our drab, suburban High Streets. A fair number seemed to feature a concoction of styles – mod, punk, goth – like something out of some mixed-up time capsule. Boys in winkle-pickers, girls in rah-rahs – often mismatched, yet faultlessly presented.

Chen Choi fitted that to a tee, even down to his early Merseybeat mop top, so impeccably coiffed that I half expected him to come out with an extended McCartney 'oooooh', whilst shaking his head vigorously.

He didn't do that, of course. Just sat there, bolt upright, in near silence. That said, when he did speak, his English was far better than Yoomi's, saying, 'Su A was my friend,' when I asked him why she'd rung him, rather than her, first.

'A close friend?' I replied, watching his eyes.

'Just friend,' he replied.

He was a cool customer all right, but had I hit a nerve?

Unfortunately, pressing the point – certainly at this stage – wouldn't tell me.

'Can you take me back to that bus trip?' I asked. 'You know – where you were all sitting.'

And he did – describing their positioning in the bus as best he could – while I visualized the layout and watched him carefully. And yes, he was probably telling the truth.

'So she just said "Mudang"?'

'Yes.'

'What did she sound like? You know, happy, unhappy?'

'Sort of crazy – like happy but maybe unhappy – I can't think of word.'

I thought for a second. 'Do you mean hysterical?'

'Yes, historical.'

'And mudang means fortune teller?'

'Yes.'

'And you've no idea why she said that?'

'No,' he said, not even shrugging.

I noticed Anna looking at her notes. I paused for a second, partly to collect my thoughts, partly to give her a chance to check whatever it was she was checking. She turned a page and then turned it back. She was looking at Yoomi's statement. Had she found something contradictory? Eventually she looked up and gave me a slight nod. No, she hadn't.

'So "mudang" is an exact translation?'

'Yes.'

'Fortune teller?'

'Clairvoyant, yes.'

'Sorry?'

'Clairvoyant. Mudang mean clairvoyant.'

Suddenly, a light switched on. Clairvoyant? Where did he get vocabulary like that? I mean, his English was pretty good, but clairvoyant? I could run with fortune teller – two reasonably common words, stuck together, with a reasonably logical meaning. But clairvoyant? It wasn't even English.

'Erm, sorry, Chen. Could you tell me – when you got the call were you able to immediately translate it, or have you looked up that word since?'

He thought for a second and then said: 'I knew this word.'

'You already knew the English word – or French, I think it is – clairvoyant? You didn't even have to think? You were able to instantly translate it?'

'Yes.'

'Where did you pick it up from?'

'Pick it up?'

'Where did you learn it?'

'Ah that easy – at the lecture.'

'Sorry?'

'At the lecture.'

'Which lecture?'

'The lecture on night before. On Friday.'

'You mean the lecture on, er …'

Anna was ahead of me, flipping back through her notebook and saying: 'English Legends, Myths and Magic by Paul Farrell?'

'Yes,' he said, only slightly turning to her.

'Right,' I said, drawing his attention back to me. 'Could you tell me about this – about what was happening when you heard this word? Take your time, think very carefully.'

And he did take his time, and he did think very carefully – and this, in précis form, is what he said:

On the Friday night before her disappearance, he, Su A and Yoomi had gone to Paul Farrell's lecture. The three of them had sat together, somewhere near the back of the hall – he to Su A's right, Yoomi to her left. Towards the end of the lecture, following questions from the audience, Farrell had written a few words on the whiteboard, explaining their meaning. Some of the words, like witch and knight, he already knew, and some of them, like warlock and clairvoyant, he didn't. The reason he remembered the latter was because they still didn't understand

Farrell's explanation and Su A had taken her electronic dictionary out of her bag and looked it up.

I found myself imagining the situation: the little screen in Su A's hand – illuminated in the darkened hall – with the word mudang on it.

'Don't you think that's a bit of a coincidence?' I asked.

He thought for a second and said, 'I suppose, but we learn new word all the time – always have electric dictionary.'

And just to prove the point, he fished the sleekest of little gadgets from his jacket pocket and showed it to me.

'OK,' I said, thinking for a second. 'Let's go back a bit. You know you said Paul Farrell explained some words to the audience at the end?'

'Yes.'

'Well, did he explain them in English?'

He looked back at me blankly. I seemed to have confused him. Then he cottoned on and replied: 'Yes, of course. All teachers only speak in English. Too many students from different country.'

'Yes,' I said. 'I know that's what teachers are supposed to do, but in this case, did he use Korean at all?'

'No, no,' was Chen's instant reply.

'Do you know if he speaks Korean?'

'No.'

'Are you saying no, he doesn't, or no, you don't know?'

'No, I don't know.'

I then asked him what happened after the lecture and he told us exactly what everyone else had – that many of the students, including he, Yoomi and Su A, had gone down to The George for a few drinks. After all, it was, as he said, a Friday night.

'And have you told the police all this?'

'About going to pub?'

'No, about the first time you heard this word – clairvoyant.'

'Don't think so, no. I just realize.'

'OK, so let's go back to that night in the pub. Did Paul Farrell go with you?'

'No, just friends.'

'Do you remember him being at the pub at all that night?'

He thought for a while: 'Yes, he come later.'

'Are you sure?' I asked, Anna and I giving each other a quick glance.

'Definitely sure, he come later.'

Clearly Farrell was going to have some explaining to do. Chen Choi was the second person to say this.

'Tell me something, Chen. Have you also not told the police about this – Mr Farrell, I mean?'

'No, don't think so. Police don't ask.'

'So just to get this right, you've never told the police about hearing the word clairvoyant from Mr Farrell and you've never told them he was at the pub afterwards.'

'No.'

'Do you think Mr Farrell could've spoken to Su A, Chen, at the pub, I mean, after the lecture?'

'Don't know. Maybe. Very crowded.'

'Well, did you see them talking?'

'Don't remember.'

Was he clamming up again? Was he beginning to feel he'd said too much already? It was difficult to say. OK, I thought, let's change tack. Maybe I should just throw him a little.

'Yoomi's a pretty girl, isn't she?'

This obviously confused him somewhat, but he simply answered: 'Yes, she pretty.'

'And Su A?' I asked.

'Yes, she pretty too,' then thinking for a second and adding, 'But different.'

'Different?'

'Yes, Yoomi tall, Su A small.'

'You don't mean Su A sexy and Yoomi not so sexy, for example?'

He looked a little upset – offended, even. 'No, not that.'
'And Su A was – is – just a friend?'
'Yes, Su A just friend.'

We said goodbye to Chen, sat back and discussed the whole
mudang thing. Did we believe what he'd just told us? We were
in total agreement on this. Yes, we did. No one was that good an
actor. So after a solid week of interviewing, we at last had a link
between someone currently at the school – Paul Farrell – and
what was happening to Su A around the time she was being
abducted. OK. It was a bit of a tenuous link, but it definitely was
a link.

What did this link tell us? Well, there were three or four possi-
bilities. First up was pure coincidence. This, of course, was
always possible. But as a detective, if you treat everything as just
a coincidence, you get nowhere.

The next possibility, put up by Anna, was that it was just
word association. The word mudang – presumably not that
common in Korea – was fresh in Chen's mind, so when he heard
Su A's cry for help, he *thought* he heard it. There again, that
possibility had been put to him time and time again. In every
interview, the first thing anyone would ask about mudang is:
'*Are you sure?*'

The third possibility, the one that was obviously uppermost in
both our minds, was that Su A was using that word as some
kind of connector to Paul Farrell. But why? Why not just use his
name?

'Maybe she'd forgotten it, you know, in all the turmoil,'
suggested Anna, sipping water from a plastic cup. 'Maybe she
was so stressed out that she said a word she knew Chen would
associate with Farrell.'

'Well, it didn't work too well, then, did it?' I said. 'It's taken
him three months to remember it!'

Anna smiled at this. 'OK, have you got any better explanations?'

'Unless she genuinely did think it was some kind of witch – which brings us back to option number one – a connection with some kind of clairvoyant.'

I then came up with a point I'd never really thought of before. It was obvious really, but sometimes you have to talk things through to work things out. 'You know what, Anna. In that lecture – myths and magic – the word clairvoyant would probably have been used in the context of witchcraft or something. Till now I've been imagining some woman with tarot cards at the seaside or writing horoscopes. But we're talking genuine witches here. Maybe a man dressed as a woman, or even a male witch – Chen mentioned something about warlock, didn't he?'

Anna agreed and said she'd do a bit of research, see if there are any covens or whatever in the area. That of course went against the grain schedule-wise – we were supposed to be wrapping the whole thing up at the end of the day.

'You know what, Anna,' I said, leaning back in my chair. 'I know I said we'd knock these interviews on the head after today, but I wouldn't mind one last shot at Farrell. I've had an idea….'

I'd just picked up my mobile to call Edward Taplow – we had no phone in the room – when, beating me by seconds, his name flashed up on the screen.

'Hi, Pamela. I was wondering if you're free for a second?'

'Just going to call you myself,' I said, 'We were just leaving.'

So Anna and I pulled on our coats, picked up our things, and closed the door on our little broom cupboard for the final time.

We walked down the now-familiar corridors to the reception area, where I left Anna leaning on the counter, having on-off conversations with Eduardo and Kirsty between their calls, and took the equally familiar stairs up to Taplow's office.

His door was slightly ajar when I got there and so, knocking softly, I pushed it open a little further. Ever the gentleman, on looking up and seeing me, he stood up, walked around his desk

113

and ushered me in – offering me a chair and asking if I wanted a tea. I accepted the chair but declined the tea.

'Erm, Pamela,' he said, looking less than comfortable. 'I, er, must apologize for calling you the other day. I shouldn't have ...'

'Don't give it a second thought,' I said, holding up my hand. 'I'm only sorry I couldn't take you up on it – perhaps another time, when I'm not so hectic.'

We then had the statutory conversation about the weather, though clearly that wasn't why he'd asked me into his office.

'Erm, Pamela. I don't want you to take this the wrong way – it certainly isn't related to my calling you at the weekend or anything – but I was wondering whether it would be possible for you to finish your work here a little earlier. You know, earlier than we originally agreed?'

Clearly this had been playing on his mind – he'd obviously been winding himself up for it. He then continued: 'You see, the police are now back here and it's becoming difficult with all these interviews ... some of the teaching staff have complained ... the pupils are being taken out of class all the time and....'

'Sure,' I said. 'No problem ... no problem at all.'

This seemed to take him by surprise. 'Oh, you're happy with that, then?'

'Yes, I was going to suggest it myself.'

'Oh, that's good ... I mean for you, if you're happy, I mean.'

'Yes, I can see how difficult it's become. I suppose you could say our job's done anyway. I mean, the police are certainly back on the scene, aren't they?'

'Certainly are,' he agreed, unenthusiastically. 'We've had four different officers in today. They're everywhere!'

He then shifted in his chair and asked: 'So what's your timescale, then? When do you think you'll be finished with us?'

'We already are. We were thinking of winding it up today.'

'Oh,' he said, looking a little surprised, though presumably pleased.

'Yes, except there is one person I'd really like to re-interview … if that's at all possible.'

'Oh yes, and who's that?'

'Well, I need to speak to Paul Farrell one last time – there's something I meant to go over with him before and never got round to.'

Taplow's face dropped. This was clearly not going to be as easy as I'd hoped.

'Ah, well, you see, he's one of the teachers who've particularly complained.'

(Yes, I bet he bloody is.)

'So you, er, don't think that would be possible?'

'Well … it's just that …'

Taplow let his sentence trail away. Whatever it was that was *'just that'*, I wasn't about to find out. Probably, it was *'just that'* Farrell was the one person the police had already interviewed half a dozen times. Or *'just that'* it wasn't *some* of the teachers who'd complained, but one: Farrell.

'Look,' I said, 'do you think it would be better if I perhaps re-interviewed all the teachers who had contact that week rather than just Farrell? It would still only be four or five people.'

'How would that help?'

'Well, tell him we've finished – which he'll be pleased to hear – but that we just need to go over a couple of tiny points with everyone. Then he can't complain at being singled out.'

He just nodded and perhaps smiled slightly.

I'd guessed right. Paul Farrell had a classic victim's mentality and Taplow, being his boss, had to pander to it.

Finally, I asked one more favour. Could he look at the languages spoken by his staff, particularly relating to Korean? Presumably this would be available on their CVs.

Job done, all I had to do now was break the bad news to Anna – we wouldn't, after all, be quitting tonight. And talking of Anna, it was a measure of how jumpy I'd become that when I got back to the reception, only to find her gone, my heart skipped a beat. The receptionists hadn't noticed her leave and it was only when I saw her through the reception windows, standing and chatting to Antoine, that I breathed a deep sigh of relief.

Anna was right. This couldn't go on.

EIGHTEEN

I'D BEEN THINKING long and hard about what Anna had said to me the day before about having no life; being too tied to my apron strings. So logically, the last thing she'd want to do would be to go on holiday with me. But truths are only things we hold in our heads. They aren't necessarily true. So yes, she found our current relationship claustrophobic – who wouldn't? But working on this case would soon be over and then she could have her life back. Unfortunately, it wasn't really about the case, it was about the situation surrounding it. How soon would that be over?

So I felt there was only one way out: Gatwick. And her going off alone would hardly be ideal, would it? I'd worry, she'd worry. As for going with friends, they were all working. That only left one option.

'Tell you what,' I said, over breakfast, 'when we've finished these interviews, why don't we go away for a couple of weeks? I'll treat you. You can look on the internet, find somewhere cheap and cheerful – you know, last minute – Canaries, maybe?'

'Oh, Mum, you can't do that.'

Now given that within minutes of her reply she was holding up beachwear in front of the mirror, I think you could translate that as 'Oh Mum, you *can do that*' – which, in truth, made me feel a whole lot happier. Anyway, I could do with a break myself.

So driving to the college that morning, despite Anna's radio choice of Kiss FM – mine would have been Silence FM – the world seemed a nicer place. And turning into the school, it was also reassuring to see just how much the police had upped their game. My normal space was taken by a panda, next to which was a squad car, next to which was a suspiciously Scotland Yardy-looking Beamer. The big guns were out.

Over the course of the morning, rumours of the police's new-found zeal spread like wildfire. Apparently, both the caretaker and principal had been woken in the small hours, escorted to the school and made to witness the going over of every room in the building plus attic, cellars; adjoining students' quarters and nearby lock-up. And during this raid, if I were to believe all I'd been told, files, boxes and a computer had been impounded.

And in keeping with this newfound keenness, just before the break I received a phone call from reception instructing me to attend a meeting with the police forthwith. Wearily, I told Anna I would, after all, be skipping lunch. On balance, though, I'd take this new zealous brand of policing over the old laissez-faire variety any day.

I still felt the need to look good in front of my ex-colleagues, though, so on the way to the meeting I stopped off at the ladies and did some hasty repair work. Then, as directed, I found my way up to the accounts office on the top floor.

The door was ajar so I pushed it open. Clearly, the dimensions of the room they'd procured, together with its faded elegance – ornate fireplace, sash windows, tall ceiling – made it one of the best in the building. And despite having shelves full of accounts files, it was still ten times bigger than the poky little hole Anna and I had been allocated.

Seated in the middle of the room, behind a huge oak desk, strewn with takeaway coffees, bacon sarnies and sticky dough-nuts, were a line of three policemen: an unfamiliar DI, flanked by the more familiar figures of Wilkins and Pollard. The whole scene reminded me of one of those old war movies where the Gestapo occupy some sleepy French village, take over the local chateau and prop their jackboots up on the Louis VIX table. I'm only surprised they hadn't ripped down the picture of the queen and replaced it with a portrait of a fully uniformed, grim-faced DCI Sullivan.

I was introduced to the mystery copper-in-the-middle – a DI McCullough – and offered a seat. Which was good of them.

McCullough, roughly late forties, was a solid-looking man with blue eyes and sandy hair, his craggy features at slight odds with his freckly complexion.

After a few pleasantries, he asked me similar if rephrased versions of all the questions that the other two had asked before. Patiently, one by one, I answered them. Then, at the end, he asked me if I had anything new – clearly the real reason for the interview.

Funny, that. The police didn't want me around, but did want my knowledge around.

I was able to give them two new pieces of information. The first related to Chen Choi's clairvoyant thing, the second to Farrell's bare-faced lies about not being in The George that night. McCullough seemed reasonably impressed with this and, credit where it's due, did at least say so.

Finally, there was one more piece of information that needed imparting. I told them that Anna and I were planning to jack it all in and jet out to warmer climes. I couldn't work out whether McCullough thought this was good or bad news. Oh yes, and out of courtesy, I also told them that we'd be doing one final set of interviews – giving him a list of whos and whens.

When I got back to our little room, Anna was in the process of Googling local clairvoyants. Unsurprisingly, so far all it had thrown up were websites offering online tarots – if you crossed their palms with online silver, that is. Oh yes, plus a website called Wicked Witches & Wenches, which she suggested we probably shouldn't revisit.

But despite her joking about this, I still felt there was a hint of anxiousness in her voice.

'Is everything OK, Anna?'

'Well, yes … but, well, I had this phone call from Ko Hyeon-gi.'

'I didn't even know he had your mobile number.'

'Nor did I. Said he'd been trying to get in touch with you, but couldn't. So he rang me instead.'

I looked at my mobile. No missed calls. Clearly he hadn't been trying that hard.

'So what did he say?'

'Well, he kind of apologized for going off on one – at you, I mean.'

'That's a result, I suppose.'

'Well, *kind* of apologized – didn't actually say sorry or anything. But I'm not sure that's really why he rang. Anyway, I told him not to worry because we're quitting the case anyway. I hope it was the right thing to do.'

'Absolutely. Saved me a job. But why do you think he rang, then?'

Anna paused for a second, looked at me and said, 'He asked me out.'

'*What?*'

'Asked me if I'd like to go out for a drink with him.'

'And what did you say?'

'Oh, come on, Mum! Hyeon-gi – what would I see in a creep like that!'

It wasn't what Anna saw in him that worried me. It was what he saw in her.

Screaming down the phone one minute, smarming up the next. The term sociopath came to mind.

And sociopath heavy is just psychopath lite.

NINETEEN

Over the next day and a half, the re-interviews panned out as follows:

Interview 1. Emma Fairclough: teacher, Su A's 9.00 a.m. lessons

Mid-fifties, local, single. Interested in amateur dramatics, a hobby that provided her alibi – being that she was at rehearsals for a local production of *Hair*. She wore a long flowing dress, with long flowing beads, long flowing hair (dyed green) and even had a long flowing face. She expressed herself in exactly the manner you'd expect from an amateur dramatist – sometimes wide-eyed and mystical, sometimes whispering and secretive, and always, in my opinion, bonkers.

Culprit factor: Zero.

Interview 2. Jo Bright: teacher, Su A's 11.00 a.m. lessons

Late twenties, local, single, recently qualified. Interests: languages and cycling.
Jo's alibi was a good one – camping with a bunch of friends. Slim, fair, and country-girl pretty. Being multilingual I asked her the obvious question – can she speak Korean? Answer: no.

Culprit factor: Zero.

Interview 3. Albert Christopher: Lecturer on the
Wednesday night

Late fifties, fairly local (Mottingham), married with young
family. Interests: Ancient Britain and football.
In our first meeting he had provided both himself and the
caretaker, Churchy, with an alibi. He had told me they
shared a passion for Charlton Athletic (if that's possible)
and that they'd also shared a car to Plymouth for a match.

Or so I thought. But this time....
'So you must've got back very late on the Saturday, then?'
'Um, sorry?'
'You and Churchy. Football matches finish around five-ish,
don't they? If you had to get back from Plymouth, what kind of
time did you arrive home?'
'I didn't go to Plymouth.'
'But you said ...'
I found myself thumbing back through my notebook, as did
Anna.

When I found my notes, technically he was right: *'Supports
Charlton,'* then a few lines later, *'Caretaker too,'* then even later,
'Went to matches together.'

I flipped forward to the notes on Churchy's interview and
they said: *'Went to Plymouth.'*

I looked back up. With his round, happy face and bald head,
he reminded me of one of those both-ways-up pictures you
drew as a kid. Turn him upside-down and all that would change
would be his expression.

'Erm, sorry, but are you now saying you *didn't* go to
Plymouth?'

'Yes,' he said, shrugging. 'I probably said I supported
Charlton – because I do. And I might've said Churchy went. But
if I did, it's only what he told me – you'll need to check with
him. We do share a car to home matches, but we're not close

friends or anything. Well, not really. We've got different interests, you see – Charlton apart, that is.'

Anna, looking as confused as I was, pushed her notepad over to me and pointed to his actual words: *'Charlton were away that day ... They're my team ... Follow them all over.'* So though he didn't actually say he'd gone to Plymouth that day, he certainly implied it.

'OK, so what did you actually do?'

'Went food shopping in the morning – Sainsbury's; always do – had some lunch, then spent some time on my computer – Detectornet, probably.'

'Detectornet?'

'Yes,' he said, smiling. 'Metal detecting site. I do that too. Ancient artefacts and stuff. Oh yes, and I would've taken Sally to the park in the afternoon. Sally's my daughter. And I always watch Final Score on the BBC – that would be five-ish.'

I honestly don't think Christopher was being evasive, or changing his story to suit the questions. I just think he was a bit vague. He certainly came across that way. But he didn't totally add up either. As a copper, you can't help but typecast people – and he didn't seem to conform to anything or anyone. Certainly not a football-supporting, metal-detecting, Ancient British abductor, anyway.

Perhaps the even bigger mystery was how he managed to attract such a young wife. But I've already told you about that old bee in my bonnet. Interesting character, though.

Culprit factor: Five. Churchy's alibi would need rechecking too.

Interview 4. Paul Farrell: teacher for Su A's 1.30 p.m. lessons. Lecturer on the Friday night

Mid-forties, local, two children, separated. Interests: rock music, occult.

As with the other interviews, I worked my way through the standard stuff, but unlike the others, half the time all I got were single-word replies – yes, no, or nothing. Then we got to the nitty-gritty.

'Mr Farrell, did you already know the meaning of the word mudang before all this hit the papers?'

He looked straight at me and shrugged. 'Can't remember.'

'You can't remember?'

'Well,' he said, 'would you? Would you remember when you first heard a word – any word?'

'That's different ...'

'Is it? Let's take ... ooh, I don't know ... let's think. Right, when for instance did you first hear the expression *nosey bitch*?'

Was I supposed to rise to this? If so, I didn't. What I did do was make a mental note of his proclivity towards the word bitch. And for the record, his answer didn't even hold water. Mudang was a foreign word. You'd be far more likely to recall first hearing that than words like nosey and bitch.

'OK,' I said, giving him a somewhat wearisome glance, 'let's stick to the English translation. You now admit that at the end of your lecture you needed to explain the word clairvoyant, or fortune teller, to Su A?'

'Yes, if you call it admittance.'

I just nodded my head and ploughed on. I did indeed. 'And you also admit that this very word – spoken by her – was all over the papers a day or so later?'

'I suppose so.'

'So why didn't you mention that to the police?'

'Because,' he said, 'I don't like the police.'

'You don't have to like them, Mr Farrell. You're not helping them, you're helping a young girl and her parents.'

After a second or two he said, 'You're talking as if you knew her. Like you're some kind of fucking expert. You never even met the girl.'

'True,' I conceded. 'I didn't. But you did. So tell me, Mr Farrell, what was she like?'

He paused, shrugged, and said: 'Just another student.'

'Another student?'

'You heard.'

'Did you er … did you *like* her, Mr Farrell?'

'What's that supposed to mean?'

'What I said. Did you like her?'

'Well,' he said, 'if I say yes, you'll say I fancied her. If I say no, it'll be some kind of hatred thing.'

I let this go. Perhaps he was right. On the other hand, for most people, there are emotions in between.

'You must have spoken to her quit a bit.'

'Of course I did, I was her bloody teacher.'

'And what about that particular night. At the pub. Did you speak to her then?'

Silence.

Then the lesson bell went. Saved by the bell, so to speak.

'Why did you tell me you weren't in the pub that night, Mr Farrell?'

He narrowed his eyes, got to his feet and left the room.

Anna and I just looked at each other, she blowing out her cheeks, me just raising my eyebrows.

Culprit factor: Eight. Over to police.

TWENTY

IT'S NOT THE arriving but the getting there. Not the rest, but the rest. Or so they say. And it's true. There's nothing like jetting off somewhere to make you forget all your woes. Slowly, another world takes over: cold car park becomes shuttle bus, becomes terminal building, becomes check-in, becomes departure lounge, becomes window seat, becomes take-off, becomes vaporous cloud – followed by blue sky – becomes holidays.

And that, pretty much, is how it happened. No hitches. No long delays or seats next to screaming babies. No lost luggage or poky hotel rooms. Just two weeks of perfect.

Mind you, before even leaving our front door, we were a little delayed by an unexpected visitor.

Anna was still upstairs trying things on and I was in the hall, so I saw the rippled shape of a man even before the doorbell went. Exhaling impatiently and making sure Anna was out of sight – she'd been wandering around semi-naked the last I'd seen her – I opened the door.

Mr Edward Taplow, no less. I didn't even know he had my home address – all correspondence thus far had been via my headed office paper.

'I'm, er, really sorry to bother you,' he said, fingering his trilby, 'but I knew you wouldn't be at the office and, well, I was coming this way and … and I wanted to catch up with you before you left.'

'Oh, er, that's all right,' I said (which it kind of wasn't). 'Do come in.'

He shuffled into the hall. I really didn't have the time or the inclination to offer him the lounge.

'I've, er, checked all the staff's CVs and I'm afraid none of them suggest they can speak Korean.'

'Ah, right, thank you,' I said.

Now I know it might be slightly unprofessional, but frankly, at that point, I wasn't that bothered. Couldn't it wait? Couldn't he just send an email?

'And I'm sure they would have mentioned it,' he continued. 'I mean, Koreans form the biggest group in our school, so it would be a real feather in their caps in their résumés.'

'Yes, exactly, they'd definitely put something like that on their CVs … Erm, thank you for that.'

There was then an awkward silence. Did he have something else he wanted to say?

'Erm, Edward, we really are running late now, so …'

'Yes, of course. Like I said, I really shouldn't have …'

'No, I'm glad you called, it's just that …'

Right on cue, behind me in the hall, Anna appeared – booted, coated and ready to go. 'Oh, hello, Mr Taplow.'

'Hello, Anna,' he said brightly, 'I was just, erm, going. Do have a nice holiday.'

'Thank you,' she said, as I ushered him to the door.

With me in the doorway and Edward Taplow on the step, he said: 'Erm, Pamela … well … I was wondering if we could perhaps get together … when you got back, that is?'

Aha! He'd phoned for a date and I'd said thanks but no thanks. And now, perhaps his last chance – I wouldn't be going to the school again – he'd decided to try face to face. Credit where it's due, it took some courage. And I must admit to feeling a tiny bit flattered.

'Of course,' I said, brushing away a wayward strand. 'We'll catch up when I get back. You can tell me how it's been going, and I can tell you about the holiday.'

I closed the door feeling perhaps slightly flushed but a little puzzled too. Where did he get my home address from?

During our journey to the airport, I mentioned this thought to Anna – me driving, her checking her make-up. 'Maybe you gave some personal details to the school before we started, or perhaps the police gave it to him?' she said.

Maybe. But I certainly had no recollection of the former, and somehow doubted the latter.

Oh well, who cared. Once we reached the airport, once the transition between home problems and holiday problems – not real problems at all – kicked in, I just let all that stuff drop. Holidays!

The break itself, though all too brief, was wonderful. Two weeks of sun, sea, sand and … no, not that. At my age, no sex is good sex. As for Anna, well, having a mother in tow was hardly going to be romantically enticing, was it? So just the sun and sea and the sand for both of us – plus a few St Miguels and Sea Breezes. But back to the case, there was one occasion – just the one – when we found ourselves discussing it in detail.

We were on sunbeds on the beach – me in the shade, propped up, reading a book; Anna, in the sun, tummy down, tanning her back – so to catch my attention all she had to do was open one eye, something she rarely did.

'Mum,' she said, squinting, 'You know that bus map – the one I put on the office wall.'

'Oh yes,' I said, putting my book down. 'What about it?'

'Well, you know there's a one-way system in the middle of Bromley where the buses go round?'

'Yes,' I said, thinking about it, but wondering why on earth she would be.

'Well, most buses don't need to go right round it, do they? I mean, most of them start at Bromley, so they only do part of it.'

Though I was much happier visualizing the blue sky, azure sea and white sand in front of me, I did give this some thought. And, for what it was worth, yes, she was right. Most buses did indeed start at Bromley North Station, so they did half the one-way system on the outward journey and the other half when they returned.

'Yes, but so what?'

'Except the bus she got.'

'The 162,' I said, my mind now fully back in the land of rain and red buses.

'Yes. It doesn't start there, does it – it goes right through Bromley – so it must go round the whole loop.'

'Yes, I suppose it does.' I shrugged, still not getting it.

'Well, that means that in one bit there must be 162s driving in the same direction, but going to completely different places.'

I thought hard. She was right. I could begin to see where she was coming from.

Anna pushed herself up and, holding a T-shirt to her boobs, sat on the edge of her bed:

'So on the same stretch, there must be 162 stops for both directions, mustn't there?'

I picked my beach bag up from next to my bed, scrabbled out my mobile and switched it to camera.

First up was the latest picture – a self-taken portrait of us both – at arm's length, smiling into the camera, sitting on our hotel balcony. I scrolled down until I got to a group of pictures of bus stops – some close-up, some wider, some sideways, some upright. In the final one – the closest of all – underneath the number 162, it said: 'Towards Beckenham.' This obviously suggested (well, obvious in hindsight) that there must be another bus stop just up the road saying something like: 'Towards Eltham.'

I scrolled back to the widest photo, and there – little more than a pinprick in the wide angle – was that other stop. Of course, I couldn't be sure it had 162 on it but I would bet my bottom dollar it did. Anna was right.

What an idiot I'd been. There again, the police hadn't fared a whole lot better. Had they checked the CCTVs on buses going to Eltham? To my knowledge, no.

*

Coming back to England from your holidays is depressing at the best of times. And this certainly wasn't the best of times: early December, cold, damp, and almost permanently dark. And driving through miserable suburbs, we were greeted by animated Father Christmases and rooftop reindeer mocking our return.

Weary, tired and cold, we finally reached home at about six – dragging two suitcases of dirty washing across a floor of accumulated junk mail.

First job: heating on. Second job: kettle. After which we unpacked cases and, ever so slowly, got back to some kind of normality.

Time was when Anna wouldn't have got stuck in – crashing out on the sofa or going straight to bed instead. But credit to her, she'd grown up a lot recently. I don't think this was down to the university years, more the years since: jobs, running a flat and maybe even helping me over the previous few weeks.

One thing I was mentally holding my breath on was what might turn up in the post, email and voicemail. For that reason I made sure I checked all these before Anna. And the good news was that none of them threw up anything significant – apart from another money transfer from Ko Hyeon-gi – suggesting, perhaps, that he still considered us to be on the case. Which I, incidentally, didn't. Oh well, never look a gift horse in the mouth.

Neither of us acknowledged the fact that I'd checked the post in semi-secrecy. I'm sure she had the same fears, but like me, they remained unspoken.

Finally, we sat down to a tea of beans on toast, plus a final drop of holiday wine, before going to bed, exhausted.

The next day I was up early, as usual, and Anna wasn't – as usual. Perhaps that's the one relic of her teen past she'd hold on to forever – unless or until she ever had children of her own.

Once dressed, made up and coffeed, I went to the office – a statement in itself. Before going on holiday, I would never have left her in the house alone, even to pop a few hundred yards down the road. Now, with the case two weeks behind us and nothing untoward in the post, it didn't seem so bad.

The weather was sunny, if cold, so I walked. I must confess that the weather conditions weren't the only reason I'd left the car behind – there was a precautionary element too. Leaving my car outside the house suggested I was in, and that Anna had company. So despite everything, I suppose I still had my fears.

Rather than ducking straight into my office, I decided to catch up with my downstairs neighbour.

Paul Dyson, proprietor of Paul's Pets, was pretty much as I'd last seen him – tan-coloured overall, jeans peeping out below, sweeping a sawdusty floor. He paused his work and asked how I was. I said fine; he said I looked it. He then told me about the terrible weather they'd been experiencing. I must say, both observations pleased me. Coming back to nice compliments and bad weather reports is all part of the package deal.

I then asked him about business; he said it wasn't good but should hopefully pick up for Christmas. He asked me about mine and I said so-so. I'd done all I could on the Korean girl thing and was now hoping for a few nice divorces. He laughed, said he couldn't help me with that, and we said our goodbyes.

I was just about to leave – opening the door with its rusty ring – when he said: 'Oh yes, someone was asking after you, a while ago now. Must've been round about the time you left.'

'Oh yes?' I said.

'Yes, a young lad, had an accent – Spanish, or Italian, maybe – quite tall.'

'Sure he wasn't French?' I asked, immediately thinking it could be Antoine (my brain auto-attuning to anything Anna).

'No, I don't think so.'

'Curly hair?'

'No. Straight and dark, I think.'

It certainly didn't sound like Antoine.

'So what did you tell him?'

'Nothing really – said I didn't know where you were.'

'Thanks,' I said and left it at that.

I left the shop, made for my office door, turned the key, pushed it and immediately hit an obstruction. A sudden shiver ran through me – plus mental pictures of severed pig's heads and mutilated cats. Too many cheap holiday thrillers, perhaps.

Pushing harder, I realized that the obstruction was nothing worse than a pile of junk mail even bigger than the one that had greeted me at home. I bent down and sifted through takeaway menus and minicab flyers etc. and found just two proper letters. Relief: both were utility bills. Good news dressed as bad. Finally, I made my way up the stairs to the landing.

I unlocked the door, pushed my way into my office and switched on the light. No blood-scrawled graffiti, no smeared excrement, and all exactly as I'd left it, if dustier. Facing me was the bus map Anna had spoken of and I couldn't help but go straight to it. Yes, she was absolutely right, the 162 did indeed go round the one-way system in a complete loop.

I walked up to the windows, opened the blinds – wintry tree-tops – then took off my coat and hung it up. I sat down, switched on the computer and, while it was warming up, played back my phone messages.

There were just three. The first was just a lot of scrabbling, followed by some muffled speech, followed by silence. Because of my uneasy state, my instant reaction was to think that it could be him again. But I played it back and decided it was probably just someone misdialling.

Message number two was a woman by the name of Anne Tracy enquiring about my services. She had a 'bit of a concern' about her partner and wanted to know if I could help her. I scribbled down her name and number on my desk pad.

Message number three: '*Hi, Mrs Andrews. This is Eduardo – the receptionist at the school. I did call round but there was no one in. I'd like to speak to you if I can. Please get back to me at the school if you can. Many thanks.'*

So that's who it was. I pictured the scene: Eduardo calls my mobile, but can't get through. So he calls the office, gets voice-mail, but declines to use it. Next, he drops by, only to find my office closed. He then makes enquiries at the pet shop below, but that too gets him nowhere. So after all else had failed, he phones my office again and leaves a message. Now that sounds like a man who's got something on his mind. But what? Oh well, only one way to find out.

I wrote his name and number below Anne Tracy's.

After thinking for a while, I got up, made myself a coffee and dusted down my computer (literally). If I'm being truthful here, there was an element of time-killing in all this. What I really wanted to do was ring Anna, see if she was up, make sure no one had suddenly whisked her away in the single hour she'd been out of my sight. But of course, I didn't. The whole point of going on holiday was to get back to some kind of normality.

I considered ringing Eduardo, but didn't. I had to think about the wider picture; had to think about Anna before getting straight back into all that stuff again. Whatever Eduardo's problem was, I thought, I'd simply tell him to contact the police. Then I toyed with the idea of ringing the police myself to tell them about Anna's 162 bus revelation. But again, I didn't. I couldn't quite stomach all that yet.

I was on the verge of finally ringing Anna when my mobile rang. Thank God, that'll be her.

But it wasn't. From the screen, I could see it was the school.

I pressed the green button, put it to my ear and fully expected it to be Eduardo. But again it wasn't.

'Hi, Pamela, how was the holiday?'

Taplow again! Not wasting time, is he? Visits us five minutes before we leave, phones the minute I get back.

'Fine … er, lovely … And how are you?'

'Oh, I'm OK, muddling along. Police everywhere.'

He then asked me about my holidays, and I gave him a brief, sun-soaked rundown, before he got back to the purpose of the call:

'I was wondering if we could meet up tomorrow evening.'

Blimey, he *is* keen.

'I'm, er, not sure I can make that.' (Never agree a first option.)

'Wednesday, then?'

'No, I've got something on.' (Total lie.)

'Well, um, when …?'

'Um, let me think … Thursday would be OK. I never have much on a Thursday.'

'Thursday it is. What time would be good for you?'

'7.30 maybe?'

'Sounds good. I'll pick you up – I mean, if you want me too, that is.'

'Yes, that would be fine.'

'7.30 it is.'

And that's how we left it, and I must admit to feeling just a tiny bit elated. And Thursday was perfect on all fronts. Back from holidays the best part of a week, so assuming nothing nasty happens in the meantime, I could surely start to think about leaving Anna alone. Talking of which …

It rang just three times before she answered: 'Hi, Mum.'

'Hi, babes, did you have a good sleep?'

'Great. And guess what?'

'What?'

'I've got another job interview. On Thursday. And it's a really good one!'

'That's terrific news! I didn't even know you were still waiting on any replies.'

'I wasn't. They just contacted me out of the blue. You know what media's like. I suppose word got around.'

'Even better. Well done.'

TWENTY-ONE

BACK FROM HOLIDAY two days; the case just kept pulling me back. Yes, I know I'd said I wouldn't ring Eduardo, but I felt I just had to. Whatever he was ringing about was obviously important to him. As for me just passing his message on to the police, no. If he'd wanted the police, he'd have rung the police.

'Ah … Hi, Mrs Andrews, how was your holiday?'

'Wonderful. Good to get away, re-charge my batteries. How about you?'

'Oh, I'm fine too. Thanks for returning my call. I hadn't realized you'd gone away.'

'So, er, how can I help you?'

After pausing, he spoke in a noticeably more hushed voice: 'Well, er … it's not easy …'

'OK,' I said. 'I understand, you've got someone near you. (In my mind's eye, I pictured Kirsty.) Would it be easier if we met up somewhere?'

'Yes.'

'Right, when's good?'

'After work would be best.'

'What time?'

'About 5.30 maybe? At the, er … let me think … do you know the Foresters?'

I noted that he didn't suggest The George, the main student hangout.

'Yes, halfway down the High Street.'

'That's it.'

'OK, the Foresters at 5.30.'

From then on, the day panned out pretty much as planned – housework, food shop, back-to-normal stuff. But I'm afraid I did tell Anna a bit of a white lie on the Eduardo front. I was feeling a little bit guilty about getting back into the whole interview thing, I suppose. I considered being straight with her, but didn't. After all, it was only one last meeting. Then I could impart any information I got to the police – given it was of any value – and have done with it.

So in the end, I just told her I'd had a phone call regarding a relationship case, which was true, and that I had a meeting lined up just after five, which was also true. What's wrong with that?

Anyway, it would do her good to be on her own. Leaving her for an early evening meeting would be yet another loosening of the apron strings. She seemed to be opening up her own social life more now too – I'd noted a hushed phone call from Antoine earlier in the day.

The Jolly Forester is a typical no-frills boozer. Sky Sports, flashing fruit machine, gnarled drinkers propping up the bar. Not the kind of place I'd use, and hardly surprising the students didn't either.

I spotted Eduardo the moment I entered, seated at a corner table, next to a large blackboard headed 'Today's Specials', which was totally blank.

Wearing a red zip-up and smartish jeans, he came straight over to me, covering the barroom in about four strides, gave me a boyish smile and thanked me for coming. He asked me what I'd like to drink and I opted for a Coke.

He then had to negotiate the buying of my drink between the bar-bound regulars – not an easy task – while I stood back a couple of paces. Finally, drinks in hand (he chose beer), I followed him back to his table.

He asked me about my holidays – which I said were great, but now long forgotten – and I asked about his receptionist work at the school, which he said was going OK. This could have led onto his reason for ringing me, but didn't. Instead, we indulged in a bit of small talk about his family in Italy. Then he came to the point:

'I need to tell you something, Pamela.'

'Oh yes.'

'It's about Chen.'

'Chen Choi?' I said, not particularly surprised, but trying to sound it.

'Well, yes,' he said. 'I've never mentioned it before, because … well, I suppose it's private really, but I think that now it's gone too far. To put it bluntly, we … I mean, Chen and me … we were …'

Suddenly, I realized. How bloody obvious! That look in Eduardo's eye when he'd mentioned Chen's name. As a detective, I should have picked that up ages ago. He and Chen were lovers.

'OK,' I said. 'I think I know what you're saying. But I don't see what that's got to do with me – or more to the point, Su A.'

'Well, it had quite a lot because … you see, she was, well …'

'She was what?'

'Well, she and Chen were …'

'Sorry, Eduardo, are you saying that Chen was your boyfriend *and* Su A's?'

'Not exactly, no. At least, Su A might have seen it that way. But I know Chen well. Well, obviously I would, wouldn't I? And he's not bisexual. But I think he was just a bit confused – maybe putting on a bit of a front, you know, flirting with her, making out he was straight. You see, it's still a big deal in Korea. His parents would be shocked. So I suppose he wanted to pretend, you know, make a bit of a show of it.'

'OK, I've got that. I could see how that could happen. But what's it got to do with the case? Are you suggesting Chen's somehow involved?'

'No, no….'

He paused again.

'Look, Eduardo, are you two still lovers?'

He looked down at his hands. 'No, not now.'

'OK, so this isn't some kind of a get-back, is it?'

'Get-back?'

'I mean like revenge. You're not telling me this now just because you've fallen out?'

He looked genuinely upset at this. 'No, no. I wouldn't do that. It's because … well … It's because you and the police have spent all this time wondering why Su A rang him first.'

Fair point. For that reason alone it's something we should have known about a long time ago.

'Plus the fact he and Su A had quite a few … well, sort of dates. Only in the park and stuff – he's never mentioned them to anyone. I think he's always been worried that it would …'

'It would what?'

'Well, how do you say in English? Open a can of worms?'

'OK, now I get it. He's kept quiet about all this because he thought it would eventually lead to everyone finding out about you and him and her?'

'Yes.'

'And then his parents would find out.'

'Yes.'

I left it a bit, hoped he would continue, but he didn't.

'OK,' I said. 'What did Su A think about all this?'

'Oh, she didn't know about Chen and me.'

'How do you know?'

'Well, I don't. But I'm sure Chen wouldn't have told her. Why would he?'

I was less sure. I could fully imagine him mentioning it in some kind of outburst – or perhaps if she wanted to take things further and he didn't, couldn't – and then him telling her the reason why.

'Eduardo … Was Su A in love with Chen?'

He said nothing, which told me lots.

This was indeed important. A girl is secretly in love. The man she's in love with does not, or cannot, reciprocate her feelings. Unrequited love: songs are sung about it, books written about it, tragedies told about it. The stuff of runaways and suicides – even murder.

Had we been looking in the wrong direction all this time? Personally, I doubted it. I still felt there was someone else involved. If she'd just taken off, where to? She didn't have her passport with her, had no friends and knew little of England. And anyway, someone would surely have reported seeing her by now. Suicide? No way. For that you need a body. That left murder. Could Chen Choi have done that? It didn't seem plausible.

He did, I suppose, have sort of a motive. She could have threatened to tell the world about him, he could have panicked and, during a row, killed her – accidentally or otherwise. He could then have made up the whole mudang thing too. Fortune-teller phone calls certainly have a whiff of fiction about them. But if he did kill her, it would have to have been after they'd separated – after all, he and four friends left her at the bus stop. So even if the mudang call was fictional, the bus journey afterwards wasn't. So if she wasn't dead, could Chen Choi therefore be holding her? Even more ridiculous. Firstly, why? Secondly, where? Are we supposed to believe that a foreign student, living in a host family's house, was somehow able to hold a girl against her will for almost three months? Unless the host family were somehow involved, which seems even more unlikely. And what of the threats I'd received? Why would he do that? Maybe they could just be down to some sicko opportunist? But again, I didn't think so. They appeared to be genuine. Whoever was sending them was holding Su A.

So Chen Choi would certainly need to be re-interviewed. It would be a priority. He'd have loads of stuff to say about their time together. And maybe his lodgings would need to be turned over too. But somehow, even though it was important news, it wasn't case-breaking news. Not in my opinion. Eduardo was right about one thing, though. It did indeed open up a whole new can of worms.

I asked him if he wanted another drink but he declined. The conversation had, anyway, found its natural end. So we drank up, left the table and talked our way to the front door, where we said goodbye. I did also mention, diplomatically, that the police would need to be informed about what he'd told me. He fully understood this. We then said a second goodbye, he loped off one way, I went the other, and that was that. Except it wasn't quite.

Driving back down the High Street, I found myself two cars back from a very recognizable van. Faded red, darker where a Royal Mail logo had been, it was an old van that was parked in the school's staff car park every day of the week. Suddenly it indicated right into The George's car park. Just as suddenly, I made that decision too. Much to the displeasure of the car behind me.

As the old van pulled up to the pub's back door, I passed it and, continuing to the far end of the car park, did a swift U-turn, backed into an empty space and, facing the van, turned off my ignition. I then sat and waited.

After about thirty seconds a man got out. He went to the rear of the van, opened its double doors and, one by one, out piled four youngsters. I was pretty quickly able to identify them as two boys, two girls, all Asian and, unless I was very much mistaken, all students.

Now one thing I could immediately say about this is that the driver was breaking the law. You can't give lifts to people in the back of old vans with no seats or seatbelts. Not a big deal, you might think – and you'd be right. However, when the man turned, and it became clear who he was, a relatively minor infringement became a grossly irresponsible act. The man was a teacher.

In a black Led Zeppelin T-shirt and unzipped motorcycle jacket: Paul Farrell.

After a few more seconds, the front passenger door opened and out hopped a sixth person. A young Asian girl – Japanese or Korean – of about twenty years of age.

What happened next threw this little cameo into an altogether different light. Before following the other four students into the pub, Farrell walked round to the girl's side of the van and, running his hand up the girl's leg, kissed her. Nothing illegal in that, of course: they were both consenting adults. Trouble was, they were consenting adults with a twenty-year age gap.

I found myself wondering what Edward Taplow would make of it all – assuming he didn't already know, of course. Oh well, he'd certainly know by Thursday night. A good topic for a first date, maybe?

Farrell and the girl disappeared inside the pub.

I was just about to switch on my ignition when the door reopened. Out came Farrell again. This time he was trailed by a couple of different lads – not Asian, but European – possibly French or Italian.

While the two students stood a respectful distance away, he opened the driver's door, ducked into the cabin, and seemed to be rummaging around for something – possibly in the glovebox. A second or two later he was out and the boys drew immediately closer.

Now what I saw next I'd been trained to observe a million times before. I won't tell you exactly what they were doing because I can't be certain. But let me describe it. The boys handed over some money, Farrell folded it into a wad and put it into his zipper pocket. He then handed them two small packages that they carefully inspected. They then put the packages into their pockets. Now, what do you think?

Then I made an error. Maybe it was because I was running a bit late – I'd promised to be back for Anna. As they re-entered the pub, I turned on my ignition and with it on came my headlights – shining directly onto the frosted glass of the pub's back door.

The door instantly reopened and Farrell stuck his head out. Whether he saw me, or recognized the car, at that point, I couldn't say.

TWENTY-TWO

HAVING WOKEN EARLY, I found myself going over and the previous night's scenario again and again. Was there a connection with the Su A case? Very possibly – it certainly explained why he was so coy about admitting being in the pub that night. Why, after all, do people like Farrell deal in drugs in the first place? The money's a factor but it's not the main one. Like his ponytail and his T-shirts, it was more likely to be a case of wanting to be down with the kids – the students. Particularly the girl students, like Su A. So that begged another question: was she doing drugs too? Again, possibly.

In an ideal world, I'd like to have discussed all this with Anna. But I'd been economical with the truth about the meeting with Eduardo and that sort of precluded my witnessing the events that followed. I wasn't supposed to be anywhere near The George. The Su A case, with all it entailed – particularly the threat towards Anna – was now supposed to be a thing of the past. Anna had her interview and her future to think about.

The police, however, would certainly have to be told.

I showered, dressed and went downstairs. Then I got myself a coffee and after a while decided it was probably a civilized enough hour to contact Bromley nick and get someone half competent.

After a couple of transfers I finally found Pollard, who said he'd mention it to McCullough, who'd probably want a meeting with me. That idea rang a few little alarm bells. I could hardly be having a discussion with McCullough within Anna's earshot.

So I asked Pollard where McCullough could be contacted and he said the school.

I phoned the college, got through to McCullough – who asked me about my holidays (I'd pretty much forgotten them) – and he suggested I come round at about midday, which certainly worked for me.

Yawning and stretching, Anna eventually appeared at about eleven. I told her I had to go out and do a few bits. Well, I did, didn't I? She said she might go for a jog before breakfast. I thought that was an excellent idea. We were both getting more and more back to normal – more and more independent of each other. ·

As I drove to the college for the umpteenth time, I must confess that I wasn't exactly unhappy to be back on the case, even if only temporarily – though I'd never have admitted it to Anna. I suppose it's just that detective work's in my blood.

Unable to park in my old spot in the school car park – that had long been procured by the police – I found another place around the back. I might add that I drove past a certain old red van in the process.

I got out of the car, huddled my coat against the wind (good luck on the jogging, Anna) and walked briskly across the tarmac.

At the reception, I purposely spoke to Kirsty rather than Eduardo. Yes, I acknowledged him, but I was pretty sure he'd want to keep his distance. And then, walking down corridors and past classrooms, for obvious reasons, I was keen to avoid Paul Farrell. Finally, climbing the familiarly creaky stairs, I didn't particularly want to bump into Edward Taplow either – I somehow felt the imminence of our date could make it mildly uncomfortable. You know, there seemed to be more and more people in that school I needed to avoid.

I didn't need to knock on McCullough's door, it was already wide open. With his sandy-haired head down – presumably studying documents – he was again seated in the middle of the room, at his rather splendid if temporary old oak desk. The difference this time was that he wasn't framed by Wilkins and Pollard. He looked up, smiled, got to his feet and greeted me. I went in, we shook hands across the desk, and both sat down.

I would guess, from both name and appearance, DI Andy McCullough was of either Scottish or Irish descent. But if he was, his accent certainly didn't betray it, being of the purest – if that's the term – Sarf London. As ever with such meetings, we exchanged a couple of pleasantries, but I did notice that he got to the point faster than most – and kept to it.

He let me do most of the talking – the sign of a good inter- viewer – and was, unsurprisingly, very interested to hear about Chen Choi's alleged relationship with Su A, and Paul Farrell's suspect nocturnal activities. But a certain look in his eye, a certain silent understanding, told me that one or both of these pieces of information tied in with something the police already knew. I would dearly have loved him to elaborate on this, but that was never going to happen. He was way too good a cop for that.

As he wound the conversation up – again, far more succinctly than most – I could kind of read his mind. He knew that I knew that he knew more. In fact the whole discussion was a meeting of minds. You know, I would have loved to have been able to wind the clock back – back to the days when I was a proper cop – just long enough to work with this man on the remainder of this case.

Walking back to my car, the weather now even colder – collar turned up, teeth almost chattering – I turned a blind corner in the car park and....

His body pinning me to the wall, his hand clamped around my neck, his face – just inches away – contorted with rage: Farrell.

'OK, lady,' he snarled, 'take this as a final warning. Stop sticking your fucking nose into my business. Got it? If I see you snooping round again, I'll ... Well, put it this way, I know where you live ... and your fucking daughter. Got it?'

TWENTY-THREE

THURSDAY. AS FAR as the Farrell thing was concerned, I decided to do exactly as he'd told me – for now. This was mainly because of Anna's interview. That too was today and once she was through that I'd tell her – *and* the police. I didn't want them questioning us about threats of physical violence just before such an important date. And talking of dates, I had one of my own. So likewise.

The day started with a hairdressing appointment and by the time I got home from that Anna was up, already trying on outfits. We had a good time – she in front of the mirror donning and discarding outfits, me fielding endless wardrobe questions: *Earrings too tarty? Lipstick too pale?* As the day wore on, I started to try outfits on too, though perhaps less fervently – my assignation being just a date, hers a career.

We had a few laughs too. At one point, trying on a top that perhaps revealed more décolletage than was prudent, Anna mischievously said: 'He'll be expecting more than just a goodnight kiss, Mum.'

'He can expect all he likes,' I replied, eyeing myself in front of the mirror. 'Expecting and getting are two different things.'

'So you won't be packing me off to the pictures tonight, then, for rumpy pumpy on the sofa?'

'It's a first date, Anna! Anyway, just buffing a bit of bodywork doesn't mean it's coming out of its showroom!'

She laughed at this. 'So no bonnet lifting, then?'

'Correct. Tonight, my bonnet will remain unlifted and my showroom locked.'

*

Anna's interview was at 4.30 in central London so she would be leaving well before my final decisions were made. But as I've said before, I value Anna's opinions – and her wisecracks – and that's why I was trying on a few bits while she was still around.

For her part, she finally settled on the same trouser suit she'd started off with, lipstick which I felt was, if anything, a little too pale and earrings which were opposite – rather too dangly. I didn't press these points, though. Sometimes she just won't be told.

At the front door, I kissed her goodbye, wished her good luck and told her she really ought to have something more substantial when she got to London – all she'd eaten was a yoghurt.

Finally, I closed the door and, with the house back to myself – bathroom, wardrobes, mirrors – got back to work. This would have been about three o'clock.

I then remember giving a brief thought to her at cup-of-tea time, because that's roughly when her interview was.

I made my final wardrobe decisions at sixish, and yet again caught myself thinking about her. Her interview ordeal would be well and truly over and I was itching to know how it went.

Prior to that I'd showered, re-dressed, tried on a number of lippos and applied my final touches. Yup, I remember thinking, not too bad for an old 'un, though the morning's expensive hairdressing had lost some lustre.

So once I settled down, mobile beckoning me from the coffee table, I found myself wondering if I should text her. No, perhaps not. Give her some space – she'll contact me if she wants to – she's probably gone out for a drink afterwards. She's got loads of friends up there.

Edward arrived right on time, looking smart in a jacket and tie, and we made our way. He had a decent but not flashy car (Volvo) and drove in a calm and unhurried manner – utterly the opposite of myself. We went to the nearby village of Chislehurst, somehow managing to park right in front of the restaurant – again, something I can never achieve. I remember being especially thankful for this because my shoes were already crippling me; I was looking forward to kicking them off as soon as they were sub-table.

Walking through and being shown to our table, the place seemed to be pleasant and unpretentious, the waiter welcoming but not overbearing. The starters made sense – though we skipped them – and my seafood pasta turned out to be excellent. We even had a gooey pudding between us – plus two spoons. All very romantic. Most of all, though, the conversation was good. I was particularly impressed by Edward on this front because, being the driver, he didn't touch a drop of alcohol: putting up with my Pinot babblings can't have been easy. Oh yes, and talking of loose tongues, in the end I decided against bringing up the whole Paul Farrell thing. It somehow seemed inappropriate. I did find out one very interesting thing, though, especially given what was to happen straight after our date.

'Anna and a lad from your school – Antoine's his name – seem to be getting on well,' I said, before taking a sip from my tiny espresso cup.

'Oh yes, I know Antoine,' he replied. 'Belgian lad, tall, curly hair.'

'I'm impressed,' I said. 'How many students …?'

'Ooh, about 280 right now …'

'And you know them all by name?'

'No, but he's slightly different – sticks out from the crowd because he's not using one of our host families.'

'Is that normal?'

'No, but we do get a few. He's got a cousin living nearby and he's staying with him.'

Suddenly I found myself wondering.

'So, er, he could have been in this area before his enrolment date?'

'Most probably, yes.'

A tiny alarm bell went off in my head. I'd never bothered to question Antoine because he'd joined the school the Monday after Su A's disappearance. But now I find he was probably here at the time.

It wasn't a big deal; it didn't incriminate him in the slightest. But it must have been sobering enough to jolt me back to thoughts of Anna and her interview. Had she phoned? Had she texted?

I excused myself, leaned down from the table, scrabbled in my bag and pulled out my mobile. I checked it for missed calls or messages. Nothing. I looked at my watch: just after ten.

Now don't panic, Pamela, it's still early. There were a million reasonable explanations. She was always going to be home a little later than she'd said – probably had drinks with friends, then realized it was too late to phone. I am on a date, after all!

I told Edward that I really should be getting back and, probably sensing something in my eyes, he asked me if everything was OK. I just nodded thoughtfully.

I took my bag to the ladies' and phoned Anna's number. All I got back was an unobtainable tone – no voicemail, no nothing. I'd never got an unobtainable before. I dialled again, got the same. So I phoned my home number. It rang and rang and finally clicked to voicemail. I didn't bother with a message.

By the time I got back to the table he'd paid the bill. I offered to split it, but he said no. I thanked him and asked the waiter for my coat. I can't have been very good company around this time because I can hardly remember saying anything to Edward.

It had just started to rain outside and, standing at the restaurant door, he asked me if I'd like him to fetch a brolly from the car. I said no. It was only a few steps. Frankly, I no longer cared about my hair.

We drove back through the night to the accompaniment of soft classical music, intermittent sweeps of the car's wipers and precious little in the way of conversation.

As we pulled up to my house, I was hoping for a few lights

on. Anna had never been an early-to-bed type and would surely want to tell me all about her interview – and hear about my date. But the only light on was on a timer switch.

At this stage panic set in and my memory begins to get a bit blurry. I must somehow have run ahead of Edward – despite wearing impractical shoes – possibly before he'd even parked up properly. I then remember scrabbling in my bag for my keys, pushing the door open, calling out Anna's name and hurrying through the house checking every room: lounge, kitchen, Anna's bedroom. Edward must have followed me into house because he was standing in the hallway when I got down the stairs. He asked me if everything was all right. It clearly wasn't, but I said it was, telling him rather lamely that it was no problem, Anna had a habit of coming in later than she'd promised – she'd be bound to turn up soon. He obviously didn't believe me. After all, if this was such a regular occurrence, why react like this?

So Edward left a little bemused – for him, a strange end to what must have seemed an otherwise good evening. And you know, I don't even recall saying good night. I must have seemed incredibly rude. All I do know is that I found myself alone in the house, knotted with fear, full of anxiety.

With my coat still on, seated on the edge of the sofa, I repeatedly pressed the green button on my mobile and repeatedly got the same tone back. This was getting me nowhere. I had to stay calm, had to think. Although I didn't hold out much hope of her being within this area, I tried a few of her local friends anyway.

The first number I tried was one of Anna's old school friends called Anneka, but all I got back was a message saying her mobile may be switched off – not unreasonable at midnight. The next number I had was a girl called Becky. I was just going to ring her when I remembered Anna saying she was on holiday this week – with another friend called Emma, the final contact I had.

Forget local friends. What I really needed was the number of one of Anna's ex-work colleagues. I thought and thought, then remembered that I did once get an email from a girl called Phoebe – Anna's best contact amongst her media set. It was about some charity fun run I got involved with. Now I was pretty sure that if Anna had gone out for a drink after the interview, Phoebe would be in on it – or if not in on it, would at least have heard about any get-togethers.

I got up, took off my coat, went over to the dining table where my laptop was sitting, opened it up, switched it on and got myself into my Hotmail account. Eventually I found the old email with Phoebe's phone number on it.

By now it was probably about midnight, but I was beyond caring about other people. So I dialled and waited. It rang and rang. At any second I expected it to switch to voicemail, but then a sleepy female voice answered.

'Hello.'

'Is that Phoebe?'

'Yes, who's that?'

'I'm really sorry to ring you so late, but it's Anna's mum here – you know, Anna Andrews – and I was wondering if you've seen her tonight?'

'Er, no, I ...' Rustling sound. 'I er, haven't seen her for a while.'

'Right, so you wouldn't know anything about an interview she had today?'

'No ... I don't know anything about that ...' Grappling sound, then click of a light switch. 'Has something happened to her?'

'No, no,' I said. 'Don't worry. I really shouldn't have phoned you so late ... everything's OK ... really.'

'Can I do anything to help?'

'No, no, it's OK. I'm er, sorry to disturb you ... I'll tell Anna to give you a call when I see her – but not tonight, of course! I'm er ... like I said, I'm really sorry....'

'No, no, it's no problem ... If I *do* hear from her I'll obviously....'

'Yes, of course … good night, Phoebe. Again, sorry to call so late.'

My next call was to the police.

TWENTY-FOUR

THE NEXT 48 hours, before the story really broke, was just a vague haze of sleeplessness and worry. Night time was spent going over and over the same old ground – beating myself up with the shoulds, ifs and maybes. Daytime was spent talking with the police, phoning Anna's friends, doing anything that could help – which in truth, wasn't that much.

My very first call to the police, at about half past midnight, was an absolute farce. I got through to the front desk where some twelve-year-old bobby asked me the missing person's name: Anna Andrews. He then asked me her age: twenty-four. Next he asked me how long she'd been missing: about eight hours. I could tell he was becoming increasingly doubtful – amused even. Personally, I found nothing amusing about it at all. Finally, he asked me where she went to, and I said the West End – at which point he became downright sarcastic.

OK, I'm aware that a fully grown woman going AWOL amongst the bars and discos of the West End doesn't call for the SAS. I'm not stupid. But this case was different. And what angered me most was the patronizing way he actually agreed with that: 'Yes, ma'am, I do realize your daughter's different – and if you could get back to us in perhaps just a few more hours.' But I kept telling him this case really *was* different. She wasn't just *any* daughter. I could almost hear his thinking: '*My daughter's not just any daughter.*' Yes, darling, that's what they all say.

Over and over again I told him about the threats we'd had,

but he just kept asking stupid questions. What finally flipped me was when he asked if 'she'd gone to a hen night or something'.

I just lost it. I told him – well, screamed at him – that I was going to report his behaviour to his boss, saying I would call DCI Sullivan, 'of whom I'm a personal friend'.

Now that, as a copper, was the one angle I used to absolutely hate other people taking with me. I'd heard all that 'Do you know who you're speaking to?' stuff about a million times over.

In the end, I never did get to call Sullivan. The desk sergeant must have mentioned it to someone who realized its importance. About half an hour after I'd put the phone down – just as I was seriously considering waking Sullivan from his slumbers – a siren, screaming down the hill from Bromley, plus a flashing blue light illuminating my sitting room curtains, heralded the arrival of the boys in blue.

I was at the door in seconds, thanking them for coming so quickly, ushering them into the lounge and asking if they wanted a cup of tea or coffee or something – anything.

You know, it's amazing how quickly you become a victim. So many, many times I'd been the one in control – walking in and sitting down authoritatively, whilst some poor sufferer was busying themselves opening doors and boiling kettles.

I half knew one of the coppers, a PC Green, but not the other, a WPC Wendy Stoddart who was so young it sort of made me think of my Anna all the more. Neither of them had any connection to the Su A case – which was fair enough – but they were reasonably well briefed, listened to what I had to say, took notes and asked me a few questions.

Mostly, they just wanted to know about the whens, wheres and whys. All I could tell them was that I had a vague memory of her mentioning a documentary film production company called either Tempo or Tempest or something. Either way, Anna had said they were pretty major, so they should be pretty easy to track down.

And that gave me an idea. God knows why I hadn't thought of it earlier. After Green and Stoddart left, I was able to occupy myself by Googling possible names. And bang, that was it: Template! They were in Charlotte Street – that too rang a bell. I couldn't see anything on their web page about recruiting though. There again, media is famously word-of-mouth. So I rang the police and told them to pass that message on.

What remained of the night – I certainly couldn't sleep – consisted of more room pacing, more attempts at her number and more cups of coffee. But the cruellest thing of all is hope. The tiniest of noises that could, just, be Anna coming home, but turn out to be a whirr of a milk float, a clink of a bottle or a car parking nearby.

Eventually, with dawn turning to day and silence turning to traffic, I could wait no longer and rang the police again. Apparently they were right on the verge of coming round anyway, so they said.

It was just before 10.30 when they turned up. And this time it was Wilkins and Pollard.

They took off their hats, followed me to the sitting room and plonked themselves down on the sofa. I offered them teas, they both declined, and I sat down opposite them.

They kicked off by asking me pretty much the same questions that Stoddart and Green had asked: times and places. This could be perceived as a bit worrying – the left hand not knowing what the right hand was doing – but I knew enough about police procedure. Firstly, they were confirming the facts and checking that my memory could be relied upon. Secondly they were taking things step by step.

But once I'd answered their initial questions, I asked if they'd had any luck with Template. Yes, said Wilkins, they had. But the bad news, the really bad news, was that Anna definitely hadn't been there. They had a strict signing-in policy, and no Anna Andrews had been recorded. They also had no record of her appointment and weren't recruiting anyway.

The inference was obvious. Someone with enough knowledge of Anna's ambitions had found details of a well-known production company (probably, like me, on the internet) and called her. And she, like me, had fallen for it – hook, line and sinker.

This brought up the issue of who would have such information about her. Well, there were plenty, I said – she had loads of friends – but not too many people who also had a connection with the school and the Su A case.

Number one on that list would be Farrell, and I told them of my encounter with him the day before. They were more than a little surprised I hadn't reported it when it happened, making me feel all the worse for not doing so. I then told them about Antoine. He and Anna had been looking increasingly like an item of late. I also mentioned the statistical quirk in his enrolment.

Next I mentioned the receptionist, Eduardo – frankly, I was past caring who I accused of what – being the only person I knew Anna had discussed her job-searching with. And while I was at it, I also told the police that Eduardo should be an early port of call for a completely different reason. He had some interesting information about Chen Choi – who in turn, would be another person worth speaking to – Su A, Eduardo and Chen Choi apparently having had a bit of a *ménage à trois*. At this point Wilkins raised his eyebrows, and Pollard raised his head from his notebook.

Albert Christopher was another possibility. OK, he was probably the most helpful of the people I'd interviewed. He was also a doting father with both a young wife and, apparently, another baby on the way. But he didn't quite add up. Neither did his non-alibi with the school caretaker. And that brought us to Churchy himself, who, if he wasn't in Plymouth, would be worth another punt.

I even brought up Taplow, my date on the night. After all, it was that very date that took me away from the house, giving whoever it was a longer window of opportunity. The time frame would just about fit too – she disappeared in the afternoon, Taplow picked me up in the evening. No holds barred. Guilty until proved innocent.

Then there was Hyeon-gi. OK, I knew the police had already turned his house over, so for one reason or another they clearly thought he was a suspect. But since then he'd phoned up Anna and asked her out for a date, which I found rather bizarre. Plus Anna's phone threat could well have been from a well-spoken Korean – putting Hyeon-gi well and truly in the frame.

With Wilkins and Pollard now in total silence – simply taking it all in – I then went over the other stuff I'd unearthed. This included Anna's realization that the 162 bus route briefly goes to two destinations in the same street, and I even mentioned, cold case-wise, Rachel Baimbridge's disappearance at London Bridge station.

But as far as living interviewees were concerned: Farrell, Antoine, Eduardo, Chen Choi, Christopher, Churchy, Hyeon-gi and possibly even Taplow.

As big a mystery was where the hell they were being held. It's one thing hiding a single girl in a cellar or whatever, but two? All the school's buildings, cellars, lockups and outhouses had been turned over, as had the homes of at least two of the above. In saying this, I was hoping that Wilkins might volunteer further information as to whose houses had been searched, but he didn't.

I must add that I wasn't even prepared to consider the possibility of Anna *not* being held. That alternative was far, far worse.

TWENTY-FIVE

IT WAS MY sister, Liz, who first warned me. She was one of the very few people I'd told. She'd offered to come round and keep me company, but I'd said no. I'm quite an independent person, especially when I've got problems.

At the time, I was lying in bed. Some distance away my mobile vibrated into life. I'd left it on the dressing table and, in normal circumstances, wouldn't have dragged my weary legs out of bed in time. But these weren't normal circumstances.

I all but fell out of the bed, picked it up, and pressed receive. Sadly, not Anna, but Liz.

'Hello, Pam, I was, er ... wondering if you've seen the news?'

'Er, no, why?'

'Well, you may want to switch on the TV. There again, you may not.'

'Why's that?' I asked, pretty much guessing her answer.

'You're in the headlines, or at least Anna is.'

I took a deep breath. 'BBC or ITV?'

'BBC.'

With Liz still on the mobile, I found the remote.

Up on the screen came a short section of the press conference we'd given in Bromley.

There was Anna, looking professional, looking chic, looking simply wonderful. I sat back on the bed, almost crying.

The newsreader was babbling away gravely, but I couldn't catch what he was saying. All I could perceive, through tearful eyes, was my Anna – in the very same trouser suit, cruelly, she'd finally chosen for the interview.

Watching the screen, I could remember the moment vividly: us walking towards the podium together, me with briefcase, Anna with documents.

Then they cut to a later section from the same piece – the part where someone asks if it's Anna's first investigation. Anna – now in close-up – looks at the camera and says: *'It's my mum's and the police's case – I'm just helping.'*

Almost in slow motion, each tiny facial expression, emphasized and magnified.

After that, they cut to a few old shots from the original Su A case, then some new material showing the front of our house. At that point I caught the newsreader's final words: *'... from where Anna went missing.'*

I sat back on the bed, stunned, shaking and feeling physically sick.

I must have put my mobile down next to me without realizing it because the next thing I was aware of was a scratchy voice coming from it. I lifted it back to my ear. It was Liz, of course, still on the phone, asking me if I was all right.

In a daze, I thanked her, said goodbye and switched it off. I hardly needed pictures. Those images would be broadcast hourly. The images in my head were playing constantly.

I considered getting a couple of sleeping pills from the bathroom but decided against it. I couldn't afford to miss anything – certainly not a phone call.

So I switched off the light, lay back and thought.

The media, like my sleeplessness, were a necessary evil. Something I'd just have to live with. In fact if, God forbid, I hadn't heard anything in the next couple of days, I'd need to start thinking about an appeal. It might be hard, could even be tearful – though I'd do my damnedest to avoid showing any tears to that bastard. But it was a job that needed doing. But would I simply be going down the same hopeless path Su A's parents had: briefings, conferences, trying to keep their daughter's memory alive? And before them, the equally lost-looking Mrs Baimbridge, Rachel's mum? And before her, a thousand other parents of abducted children?

Finally, I must have dozed off. Fitful, maybe, but at least it was something close to sleep. Again, I was roused by my mobile – this time having remembered to place it on my bedside cabinet.

'I suppose you were fucking well asleep.'

'Er, wh ... who's that?'

'Well, you're fucking lucky, then. Thanks for keeping me informed.'

David, my ex. I really, really should have told him, but what with everything else ...

In my defence, the only contact he'd had with Anna was for birthdays and Christmases. Also, as suggested by the police, I'd been keeping disclosures down to an absolute minimum. But none of those excuses really washed. To find out that your daughter's been abducted via a TV announcer is appalling. I really, really should have thought to tell him.

Maybe, deep down, I'd avoided telling him because of the flak I knew I'd get back. He'd be bound to heap the blame on me for getting Anna involved. But if it was subconscious, it was very subconscious indeed. The last person I was thinking of at that time was a man who had walked out on Anna's life – and mine – without so much as a backward glance.

'I'm really, really sorry, David, I should've told you, but ...'

'Sorry? Sorry! Do you know what it's like, finding out your daughter's been kidnapped on the fucking news? Can you even imagine ... there again, you wouldn't care, would you? I mean, as long as you're playing the TV detective, stuff your daughter – *my* daughter. Who cares what danger she's in? I'm a big celeb now....'

'Now that's not fair, I was only giving her some work between—'

'Not fair? Not fucking fair! Who was the one who accused me, in front of a bloody court, of being an unfit parent?'

'Oh, don't drag all that up again. All we should be caring about now is Anna. All that's in the past …'

'We? Suddenly I'm involved. How can *we* be caring if *I'm* not even told?'

'OK, OK, you've made your point. It's my fault. Jesus, the media coverage was as much of a shock to me as it was to you – I only found out about it because Liz rang me late last night.'

'So why didn't you ring me then?'

'Look, I forgot. I'm sorry. It's my fault, that's all I can say.'

I let him simmer down a bit, thought for a second and then said: 'Look, if you really want to help, I'm going to ask the police to do a press conference – jog people's memories. It would help if we could do it together, show a united front and –'

'Oh, here we go again! More press conferences! Is that all you can think about – fucking press conferences?'

'OK, OK. Forget the bloody press conference. Forget everything, in fact. I've given you my apology. If it helps I'll say it again: Sorry, David. I forgot to tell you your daughter had gone missing. Is that better now? Does that make you feel better? Perhaps if you'd showed a bit more interest in her over the years I might have remembered –'

'Interest in Anna! It was you that said in court –'

I hit the red button, slammed my phone down and buried my head in the pillow.

Jesus, that's all I needed. Decade-old custody battles!

Upon reflection – upon very long reflection – he did me a favour. I felt wretched enough already, blaming myself for everything. The sudden realization that I hadn't even told Anna's dad had briefly made me feel even worse. But his ridiculously childish stance had had the opposite effect. If he'd shown just a modicum of sympathy, if he'd said something like, '*Don't blame yourself, you were only doing what you thought was right,*' I would probably, in a strange way, have felt even worse – probably even cried. But he didn't. He was just settling old scores, and that made me very, very angry.

I punched my pillow, threw myself back down again and just curled up.

You know, when women say men are useless, they're wrong. Men, or at least men like David, serve a very useful function in life. They're put on this earth to make women, or at least women like me, stronger.

TWENTY-SIX

OVER THE NEXT twenty-four hours it would have been easy to fall to pieces. But I didn't – quite. This was mainly achieved by simply keeping busy. And the man I have to thank for that was DI Andy McCullough.

He readily agreed to the idea of a press conference, though the final say would be Sullivan's. He also suggested that I could help with the checking of the tapes from the 162 buses. After all, he reasoned, there'd be no one better placed to identify staff members than me, especially on blurred video – apart from the staff members themselves, of course, but most them were suspects. There was even an outside chance it was someone from Anna's past, and I would be the best bet to identify them, too.

So whilst I would be looking out for images of staff, teachers and anyone Anna might have known, Yoomi would be looking out for her best friend, Su A. Between us we'd cover all bases.

For all that, I was still mildly surprised that Sullivan had sanctioned this – *if* Sullivan had sanctioned it. There again, I would only be helping with identification – no grilling of suspects, of course.

When McCullough picked me up at my front door – giving me a firm handshake and ducking inside my house – it gave the huddle of pavement-bound hacks the photo opportunity they'd been waiting for. We then breathed in, McCullough said 'Let's go', and, to the clicking of cameras and calls for comments, we ducked into his car and sped off to meet Yoomi.

MIKE UDEN

Andy McCullough was definitely my type of copper. No-nonsense, to the point, yet open to reasonable suggestions. And during the journey, rather than just indulge in small talk, he used the time productively, filling me in with any information he was permitted to impart. For instance, he told me that no money, as yet, had been withdrawn from Anna's account using her missing credit cards.

'Did you expect there to be?' I asked.

'Well,' he said, 'it was from Su A's account.'

'Really?'

'Yes, just after she disappeared – two hundred pounds withdrawn from an ATM in New Malden.'

Suddenly, he was ringing a few bells. New Malden was where Hyeon-gi lived. It was also a bit of a mini-Korea. This would be one of the reasons they'd turned over his flat.

McCullough found a parking place, switched off the ignition, looked at his watch and declared that we were about fifteen minutes early – then simply continued to fill me in. I found myself wondering whether he'd arrived early precisely for that purpose – to allow us talking time within the privacy of the car. After all, as a copper, I felt he was overstepping the mark in some areas. For instance, he told me that quite apart from Su A's DNA, forensics had also found traces of plants on the note.

'Viscum album.'

'Viscum what?'

'Mistletoe.'

I froze, my memory flashing back to my very first day on the case. The day immediately after the public appeal. On my doorstep, with the words 'kiss, kiss' on it, was a bunch of mistletoe.

McCullough obviously saw my face whiten, asking me what was wrong. I told him. He thought long and hard. Did we still have it? he asked. No, I said, Anna had binned it weeks ago.

We started to think of any connection to the school, but couldn't come up with anything.

True, it was December. But somehow I imagined it to be something that appeared later in the month. Around about the time of the staff party – or even the day before they closed. Like CDs of Christmas carols and receptionists with sparkly bits in their hair, it's something that wears a bit thin if it appears too early.

He then asked me if I could think of any particular connection to Farrell. I couldn't, but asked him why. I noticed he was looking at his fingers. I got the impression he was biding his time, weighing up the pros and cons of telling me something.

'Er, Pamela,' he finally said. 'We've pulled in Farrell.'

'For the drugs?' I asked.

'No, well, that as well – we found evidence in his van – but we're thinking about charging him with the abduction too.'

I was a little surprised at this. I could fully see that he was a suspect, but I didn't think they had enough on him. Not yet, anyway.

My lack of response to this news must have given my slight scepticism away because he went on to explain the CPS's reasoning:

'Firstly,' he said, 'forensic tests show that the paper comes from a batch at the school.'

'OK, but how does that specifically incriminate Farrell?'

'It doesn't, but his alibi that Saturday doesn't hold up either. He said he was with his kids. He wasn't, they were with their mum. He's now saying he can't remember what he was doing – got his weekends mixed up. And don't forget, that wasn't the only lie he told us. As you know, he was also at the pub on the Friday.'

'Yes, but that could be because of the drugs,'

'Pamela, it could *all* be because of drugs.'

'OK, but on the alibi front, he's hardly the only one, is he? I can think of at least three others who haven't got decent alibis.'

'Yes, but they haven't been threatening you, have they?'

'We only know that one of those threats came from him.'

'True, but as you pointed out, he used very similar language.

And the other point is their timing. Did you realize that all three threats just happened to be exactly one day after you'd interviewed him?'

I must admit I hadn't. I mentally went through the dates and he was dead right.

'Oh yes,' he added. 'And don't forget the withholding of information – he knew perfectly well that the word mudang could implicate him, which is why he didn't mention it. Let's throw in drug dealing and a penchant for young Korean girls and I reckon we might have a case, don't you?'

He was right; it did all begin to add up.

McCullough fell silent for a few seconds then looked at his watch: 'Right. Time for Yoomi.'

It was now raining steadily, so he turned the ignition on, drove right up to the school's front door, switched off again and, with his suit jacket pulled over his head, pushed the car's door open and ran up the steps into the school.

While he was away I looked out of the rain-streaked windows. Nope, no red vans today.

After a couple of minutes McCullough skipped back down the steps – this time with Yoomi in tow – bustling her into the back seat of the car before jumping in himself: 'Of course,' he said, brushing raindrops from his suit jacket, continuing the conversation as if he'd never been away, 'The other thing is, where the heck is he holding them?'

The way he phrased this brightened me a little. 'So you're still sure they're both, well …'

'Alive,' he said, completing my question. 'Yes, I am, and I'm not normally wrong about these things.'

This was about the most comforting line I'd heard in days. And the point is, coming from someone as forthright and no-nonsense as McCullough, I knew it wasn't just words. He wasn't the type to simply say what people wanted to hear.

'Perhaps this CCTV stuff will give us the answer,' I said.

'Yes,' he said, 'perhaps.'

TWENTY-SEVEN

ON HEARING THAT we'd be viewing the CCTV material in a bus depot, I had a mental picture of us sitting in a cramped little room, surrounded by engine parts, bits of old buses and wall calendars featuring semi-naked girls draped across tractor tyres. Parking up in an oily-floored car park, then walking through the pigeons-in-the-roof depot hadn't helped either. But by the time Alan Appleton, the depot manager, had taken us through to the administration area, we were back in officeland – white walls, vertical blinds, grey workstations.

And the CCTV images – which I'd half expected to be viewing on some clapped-out old VHS – were ready and waiting on his desktop as media files.

With his laptop turned towards us, we sat round his desk in a semi-circle, he suggesting that we should run the material chronologically. This would start with the bus that left Bromley at 3.34, a good fifteen minutes earlier than Su A could reasonably have been there; then the 3.54, which again, was slightly early; then the 4.04 which was favourite; then the 4.14; and finally the 4.24, which left well after she should have been there – assuming she ever was there.

We clicked the first file. 'This stop's Bromley North,' he said, as the image came up. 'A couple of stops before she should've got on.'

Jerky and blurred, my immediate impression was just how spooky, almost voyeuristic this all seemed. Anonymous shoppers as they went about their business; the rhythm of the cameras as they silently flicked from one to another – front, middle, rear. We were the stalkers now.

At that time, it didn't take much to trigger off the blackest of thoughts, and somehow the idea of us being voyeurs was all it took. Anna's abductor, whoever he was, had been stalking us for weeks. Had he been filming us too – poring over images of Anna, like a piece of pornography? Worse still, is he still filming her … while he …

My whole body physically shuddered at the thought. I must stop this, I told myself. Must pull myself together. Get back to the job in hand.

Being a wet Saturday afternoon, in a very busy shopping centre, the pictures showed a bus rammed full of shoppers. Passengers who could find their way to a seat were quite easy to identify. But those that stayed near the door, squeezed amongst the jostling, raincoated shoppers – arms outstretched to steady themselves – were far more difficult to pin down. Sometimes Appleton would have to go back and replay the action, placing his finger on the screen and tracing a person from camera-to-camera.

During all this, Yoomi, our spotter-in-chief, remained silent. She was a girl of few words anyway – probably because, English-wise, she only possessed a few. Also, I got the impression that, culturally, Korean youngsters – particularly girls – were discouraged from speaking their minds. So I did find myself wondering whether she'd speak up even if she did see anything.

The first file took ages and threw up nothing, despite the fact that, on one occasion, I thought I'd glimpsed Paul Farrell. But in the end, on closer scrutiny, I was just imagining things.

The second file took just as long. At one stage I thought I'd spotted Su A, but again, I was mistaken. I also found myself feeling a little embarrassed for mentioning it. A girl, clearly of Eastern extraction, got on, and without thinking, I exclaimed: 'Su A!'

Yoomi, who up to that point had remained absolutely silent, said: '*She not Su A. She not even Korean!*'

I'd fallen into the rather embarrassing trap of implying that all people from her part of the world look alike, irrespective of which country they come from. This girl was probably about as similar to Su A as I was to Jennifer Lopez. Feeling a bit stupid – and decidedly un-PC – I shut up from then on in.

This took us to section three: the favourite. With this one, if anything, we took even longer. Again we started at Bromley North, again we double-checked everything, and again we found absolutely nothing.

I looked at the clock. Almost 12.45. We'd been at it an hour.

'We could have a break, if you like,' suggested Appleton, leaning back on his chair.

No one said anything so he suggested we send out for some sandwiches and continue.

That sounded a good idea, so he left the room briefly and came back with a woman called Ruby, who had a wide smile and an even wider girth.

'What'll it be?' she asked, with pen hovering over notebook.

We ummed and ahed before she saved us: 'How about I get a mixture – they do a lovely platter over the road?'

We agreed, she left, and we turned back to the computer. File number four opened like all the others but with noticeably fewer people. Perhaps that was because the afternoon was wearing on, or perhaps because this bus didn't coincide with a train at the station. Either way, it made the viewing far easier.

At the first stop four people got on, none of whom looked vaguely like anyone from the school. Then at the second stop, the bus doors opened, and ...

'That her!' shouted Yoomi. 'That Su A! That her!'

TWENTY-EIGHT

THE IMPLICATIONS OF that discovery, not least for the police, were huge. Three months had passed since they'd pored over the bus tapes. The wrong bus tapes. And during that time, not once had anybody thought to check the buses going in the opposite direction. As a result, not only had the case gone cold, but another victim had now been kidnapped. And the irony? That other victim was Anna – the very person who'd suggested viewing the tapes in the first place.

So did this make me furious, make me want to run screaming at Sullivan, or ring up the press and expose the police's appalling oversight? No, not really. Perhaps this was because I too had missed it. And maybe simply being a victim's parent changes you. You just don't care about all that. All you really care about is getting your child back. Finger pointing could wait.

The first thing we'd had to do that afternoon was study the material in almost microscopic detail. But no matter how many times we viewed it, we found nothing new. Just a little Korean girl, standing all the way, head down and playing with either her mobile phone or a game station – which could explain why she went the wrong way for so long – whilst other people got on and off around her. Then she got off at what turned out to be Chislehurst High Street – a good fifteen minutes after she'd boarded.

We also scrutinized all the other passengers. Was anyone else from the school on it? Did anyone try to strike up a conversation with her? Did anyone even look particularly suspicious? The answer to all those questions, after much analysis, was a big fat no. In fact, when she did finally disembark, she didn't even ask the bus driver where she was. Just got off.

Driving back, sitting in silence, I'm sure we were thinking along similar lines. Su A hadn't looked particularly lost. She hadn't taken the next bus back either – which is what most people would do. So was it really a mistake? Did she, after all, know where she was going? If she did, was there someone at the school who lived in that area? Yes. The very same person who'd taken me out of the house, thereby ensuring I wasn't around when Anna had gone missing. Mr Edward Taplow. Could it really be him?

As we drove through the depressingly festive streets of Bromley, McCullough broke the silence.

'You know, perhaps I shouldn't be saying this, but there's nothing to stop you continuing to do interviews, Pamela.'

'How do you mean?'

'Well, I know how you want to stay involved – keep busy – and I'd be exactly the same myself. But even if you can't be in our interviews, I can't stop you doing your own, can I? You're a private investigator – you've been employed by Su A's parents. It's up to you, of course, but I know what I'd be doing.'

'That's a kind thought, Andy, thanks,' I said.

And it was.

'Just don't tell anyone I said it, that's all,' he added.

'Don't worry,' I said. 'I won't.'

And of course, I wouldn't. Sullivan, for one, would be dead against it. Things may have changed now, but not that much. The school wouldn't be too keen either. By now, they were absolutely fed up with the whole interview thing.

But McCullough was right. I'd only agreed to stop interviewing because Anna had wanted it. Now she was gone.

I also found myself wondering what Anna would want. Keep my distance, have a hands-off approach? Or do everything in my power to find her? The answer was obvious. Anna would want me involved. Not just for her good, but for mine.

So as we neared the school, I asked Yoomi if Chen was at the school today, she confirmed he was and so I asked McCullough if he had any objection to my speaking to him.

'Be my guest,' he said. 'Like I said, I can't exactly stop you, can I? But I would ask one thing.'

'What's that?'

'Could you avoid bringing up any new stuff? I'll be speaking to him tomorrow myself – after I've had a word with Eduardo – and I want to be the first to talk to him about the … you know what.'

'No problem,' I said. I knew exactly what *you-know-what* was. He was referring, of course, to Chen's alleged relationship with Su A – and with Yoomi in the car, he had to call it that.

I could see why McCullough wanted first pop at *you-know-what* too. If I'd already grilled him on it, Chen would get the chance to get his story right, destroying the element of surprise.

So what McCullough was doing here was encouraging me to keep interviewing people, but only on his terms. He probably guessed I'd want to get involved again anyway, so why not play the good guy and suggest it now? So yes, he was being compassionate. But he was being very clever too.

We turned left into the school's gates and pulled up outside the main entrance. With the car still running, McCullough got out of the car, opened the door for Yoomi, and thanked her for her help. She said nothing, leaving the car and making straight for the school's canteen.

McCullough got back in next to me.

'Er, Andy,' I said, 'I've been thinking, and in view of what you said, I've got a favour to ask.'

'Go ahead,' he replied, as he settled himself down.

'Well, would you mind speaking to reception – about me having a word with Chen, I mean. It'll be better coming from you and I'm not sure I can face them right now.'

'No problem,' he said, this time switching off the car before getting back out. 'Give us a few secs.'

After a few minutes he came back, stooping into my window. 'He'll be in room four, just along the corridor on the right. It'll be empty – the classes are finished.'

'Thanks,' I said, getting out of the car.

We then shook hands. I thanked him and made for the school.

'And don't forget,' he said, 'if I can be of any help at all …'

Strangely, I hadn't actually been in a classroom before, so I wasn't exactly sure what I'd find. I pushed the door open, and because the entrance was at the whiteboard end, the desks were facing me – set out in a 'U' shape, rather than regimented rows. It was all pretty basic – magnolia paint and strip lighting – plus a few pictures of the English countryside on the walls. This apart, all that was worth noting was a map of the British Isles on the far wall and, behind me, a chart showing the English phonemes. I studied them carefully. The 'letters' on it – just a load of squiggles and dots – looked like some kind of ancient runic alphabet. Straight out of *Lord of the Rings*, in fact.

I turned back to the class, pulled up the seat next to the whiteboard – presumably the teacher's chair – sat down and gathered my thoughts. The main point – Chen's relationship with Su A – was off-limits. So what else would I be asking? Frankly, I wasn't sure. I didn't, for one minute, think he was the perpetrator. But I was certain he knew more than he was letting on.

The classroom door, already slightly ajar, creaked open slightly further. Expecting it to be Chen, I got to my feet.

But poking his head round the door, with a smile on his face, was Albert Christopher.

My initial thought was that he'd come into the room to prepare for a lesson. But his greeting of 'Hello, Pamela, just popping in to see how you were' suggested otherwise.

It kind of took me aback. Most people, for one reason or another, were avoiding me. After all, *'How are you?'* is a ridiculous greeting to someone whose daughter has just been kidnapped. And even *'I'm sorry to hear about Anna'* is inadequate. She wasn't ill, and, thank God, didn't merit messages of condolence. Christopher was doing the exact opposite and I found myself wondering whether he even knew about the whole situation.

When I answered truthfully, with something along the lines of 'It's tough, but I'm getting by', he didn't react in the way I'd expect at all. Most people would include such phrases as *'Yes, I'm sorry to hear about...'* or *'It must be awful...'* or *'If I can help in any way...'* but Christopher didn't. All he came up with, rather bizarrely, was, 'I did wonder whether you might be back,' adding nothing sympathetic whatsoever.

For want of something to say, *anything* to say, I asked him about his wife and young family and he said they were fine. He then simply said goodbye and left.

I found the whole thing profoundly uncomfortable. Weird, even. OK, unlike Farrell, he'd always been helpful and maybe this was his way of showing compassion. But it didn't come over like that. It almost felt like gloating.

Perhaps he just didn't read papers or watch the news. Mind you, it would also mean he didn't speak to his colleagues either – they must surely have been discussing the Anna situation. Nope, it just didn't add up.

As my thoughts drifted I also found myself, yet again, wondering what on earth a young woman would see in a man like him: middle-aged, overweight, balding, and in possession of no social skills whatsoever. Oh well, it takes all types.

After a minute or so there was a light knock on the door. This time it was Choi. His attire, as ever, was meticulously matched. He still had his mop-top hairstyle, of course, but it was now accompanied by what I would describe as American 50s Ivy League – tasselled loafers, chinos, polo shirt and preppy sweater draped over his shoulders. All very kitsch. And all very expensive.

I stood up, greeted him, and suggested we sat at one of the desks. He went for the nearest one and I picked up the teacher's chair and put it down facing him.

I noted he didn't offer any sympathies, making no reference to Anna's abduction. I took this to be awkwardness more than anything – an extreme case of the point I've already made about people not knowing what to say. And anyway, even at the best of times he was a young man of few words.

I decided to simply ask a question I'd asked him before, to which I'd never really had a satisfactory reply: 'Erm, Chen, I still don't understand why you only recently mentioned that word mudang coming up the night before – you know, in Paul Farrell's lecture.'

As before when asked this question, he just shrugged.

'Don't you think it's a bit coincidental?'

No response.

'You see – and I hate to have to say this, Chen – it makes me wonder whether you're just making the whole thing up.'

'No, no,' he said, suddenly coming to life. 'She say mudang.' Then, after a brief pause, he casually added: 'Or something like.'

'Sorry, Chen. "*Something like?*" Do you mean she could have been saying something else?'

'Well, maybe I hear lecture man say mudang, so that what I think Su A say.'

'Right,' I said. 'You mean it could have been word association – you'd only just heard the word, so you thought that's what she said.'

'Yes, word associate.'

'So,' I asked, 'what do you think she might have said?'

'Well,' he said, sticking out his bottom lip, 'maybe mudum.'

'Mud*um*, not mud*ang*?'

'Yes.'

'And what does that mean?'

'Not sure exact translation, but …'

He put his hand in his pocket, pulled out his electronic

dictionary, fiddled with it and finally said, 'Ah yes, mudum mean tomb.'

'Tomb? You mean like grave?'

'Yes, underground, for dead people.'

Jesus, I thought. I think I was happier with the original translation.

I would obviously have to pass this onto McCullough, but it wasn't a subject I particularly wanted to delve into myself. So I spent the next few minutes trying to find out if he knew of any meetings between Farrell and Su A. This got a big fat zero, so I pushed it slightly harder.

'So neither of you bought anything from him?'

Chen eyed me suspiciously. Clearly he knew that I was referring to drugs. It must have been an open secret amongst the students.

'Mr Farrell not my friend,' he simply said.

I didn't want to go too deeply into this one either. Yet again, I was moving into McCullough's area.

'Er, Chen?'

'Yes.'

'One last thing. I don't think I ever asked you this before but, er, can you think of anyone at the school who can speak Korean – and I don't mean Korean students – I mean people like staff?'

He thought for a while and then said:

'Ah yes. Mr Taplow, he speak Korean.'

TWENTY-NINE

WHEN IT FINALLY came, I can't say exactly how I felt. I simply had too many conflicting emotions. Any scrap of evidence that she was alive was welcome, of course. But on the other hand, as intended by the sender, it was chilling confirmation of what I'd feared all along – that her disappearance wasn't just some random turn of events: Anna involved in a minor accident in the West End, where she briefly lost her purse, her mobile and her memory, then woke up in a hospital bed. Yes, I do realize that such hope sounds ridiculous. But until you have evidence to the contrary, these are the thoughts you cling to. Well, now I knew. He definitely had her. And his particular method of proving that was vile in the extreme.

It was sitting on my doormat when I got back from the school: ordinary, postman-delivered, through-the-letterbox postage. Even that was probably calculated. Just to demonstrate how in control he was. First message by phone at my workplace; second message by hand on my car; third message by post to my home. He chose time, he chose place, he chose method.

I suppose I wouldn't normally have noticed an individual piece of mail straightaway, or picked it up so quickly. Normally, the post is something to be picked up and left, kicked to the side, or simply trampled on. But there was something about this envelope: clean, neatly typed and precisely stamped. Read me, it said. I'm what you've been dreading.

I stooped down, picked it up, turned it over (nothing on the back) then simply ripped it open. Yes, I know. An ex-cop should know better. An ex-cop should lift it up by its corner, place it on

177

a worktop, carefully prise it open and deftly slide it out. But I didn't, I just tore at it.

Everything I told you earlier about my mix of emotions – relief, yet terrible despair – hit me then.

The first few fractional seconds, my eyes scanned the words at the top of the note:

BITCH

GOT YOUR DAUGHTER

LIKE I PROMISED

I then dropped my gaze. About halfway down the page was a much smaller line of lettering:

CHECK DNA ON THIS

Below this, at the very bottom of the page, was a strip of Sellotape. At first sight it didn't really register. Just a piece of dirty, apparently well-fingered tape. It could almost have been an accident. But it wasn't an accident. It was lined up too perfectly – horizontal to the bottom, centred to left and right.

Looking more closely, stuck under it was hair. Possibly human hair. But not head hair. Not a clump of hair. Not even a lock of hair. A sparse, perfectly set row of individual, dark, curly hairs. Suddenly I realized. It was obvious – sickeningly obvious. Anna's hair was blonde. These weren't.

These were pubic hairs.

I nearly wretched, vomit physically rising in my stomach. Only anger, absolute fury, prevented me from throwing up. Suddenly, all those earlier emotions were banished. Pushed aside by sheer rage.

I would kill this man. I didn't care about the consequences. Without Anna, I had nothing anyway. If he took her away from me – and maybe even if he didn't – one way or another, I would kill him.

178

THIRTY

'DO YOU WANT to call it off? asked McCullough, amongst the mêlée of police personnel milling around my house.

'No,' I said.

'Or perhaps postpone it a day?'

'No,' I repeated. 'Let's do it.'

I was shaken, of course. But I'd promised to give a press conference that day, so a press conference I would give.

My sister Liz kindly volunteered to housesit while I was out. She'd come round as soon as I'd called her – this time I really did need a shoulder to cry on – and promised to stay the night with me when I returned.

Leaving the house with McCullough, it was immediately noticeable that the group of journalists was now down to just four. Three days earlier, in the immediate aftermath of Anna's disappearance, they'd been well into double figures. These hardy hangers-on must have wondered why there was suddenly such a lot of police activity and, as we pushed passed them, they were full of questions. McCullough simply waved them away, telling them to go to the briefing – they'd find out there.

During that journey, nosing our way up Summer Hill, I asked McCullough whether he'd spoken to Taplow about his sudden ability to speak Korean.

'Yup,' he said, tapping his steering wheel, 'I was going to tell you about that. He seemed quite laidback about it. I suppose I can kind of see his point. I mean, you ask him to check the staff and that's exactly what he does – he's not staff.'

179

'But come on, if you were him, surely …'

'Maybe, but I'm not. And anyway, he said it was in relation to some re-interviews you wanted to do – something to do with their CVs. Clearly he didn't think it applied to him, so he didn't mention it.'

'Mmm,' I commented.

'In fact,' added McCullough, 'when I pushed him on it, he seemed a little offended – even told me he'd mentioned it to you on a date or something.'

'He did?' I found myself feeling a little flushed. I suppose it was something to do with it being called a date. I'd obviously told McCullough I'd been with Taplow on the night in question, but hadn't actually referred to it as a date. It kind of made it sound like we were, well …

'Yes, he said you went out for a meal together, and you had a conversation about books or something. You'd just finished some romantic novel and he'd just finished a book by some Japanese author. He said he mentioned that he reads books in a number of languages – including Korean.'

I cast my mind back. Yes, we did indeed have that conversation.

At roughly the same time as the Su A case had started, I finished reading the bestseller, *One Day*, a book that had infuriated me and captivated me in equal quantities – sometimes all but throwing the thing across the room, sometimes curled up on the sofa, lost in its lovelorn little world. In fact, the story's out-of-the-blue ending had so affected me that, even days after I'd finished it (driving in my car, or just sitting at home listening to music), I'd found myself holding back the tears. But now, confronted with true grief, it all seemed so meaningless. After all, that last time I'd recalled it, sitting in the restaurant enjoying a glass of wine with Taplow, I was just minutes from the bomb-shell. And now, sitting in the car, watching the real world slide by, I almost felt shame. Shame that I'd been so moved by it. How could I cry real tears at music and books and things, yet remain so stoical in the face of such real-life adversity?

'You OK?' asked McCullough, glancing over at me.

'Yes, yes. Fine,' I said, pulling myself together. 'Sorry, I was just thinking …'

McCullough had more sense than to ask exactly what I was thinking. It was only ever going to be one thing.

But back to Edward Taplow, he may well have been right. I do remember him telling me he was reading something in Japanese. Perhaps he was trying to impress me – men do that sort of thing on dates. But I really can't recall a conversation about Korean. There again, it was a date. We were sitting in a restaurant having a drink; I wasn't exactly taking notes. And at about that time … Well, the only thing racing through my mind once that happened, was the same thing that's living in it now.

David Sullivan, still in overall control, had arranged to meet us at the venue. He'd chosen a small community hall in Chislehurst High Street, which, in many ways, had echoes of the conference that Hyeon-gi had organized in Bromley – its proximity to all-important bus stops making it part-appeal, part reconstruction. And it was perhaps mildly ironic that Sullivan, having refused to attend the original conference, had taken a leaf out of Ko Hyeon-gi's book on this. There again, it made a load more sense than having it in some unrelated location. After all, whilst the attention we were getting was national – sometimes international – the information we needed was local.

We parked up immediately outside the hall – a squat, pebbledash building at the end of a row of shops – the police having cordoned off an area of the pavement to enable us to get through the small crowd that had gathered.

With McCullough leading the way, we left the car, strode across the pavement and pushed through the swing doors. We then made our way between the rows of chairs – empty apart from a few journalists who'd bagged front seats – to the trestle table at the head of the hall, where Sullivan, resplendent in full uniform, already stood. As cameras snapped, he greeted me with a warm hello and solid handshake. Whether that was for the benefit of me, or the press, I couldn't say, but I'd like to think it was the former.

By the time we sat down – Sullivan centre stage, McCullough and I to his left and right – the hall was packed. The briefing would be in two parts – two separate conferences, in all but name. Firstly, there were the further details of Su A's disappearance. This would be given by Sullivan, with some of the questions fielded by McCullough. Secondly, there would be information about Anna going missing – which was sketchy, at best. At this point, I would say a few words.

In the police's opinion, this distinction between the two was essential. Whilst it was important to cover the two abductions together – because they were inextricably linked – it was just as important that the respective times, dates and locations were kept separate. I must add that there could also have been a political game going on here too. The public perception, that I was somehow running the Su A case, still rankled hugely – particularly with Sullivan. And had Anna not gone missing too, I wouldn't have been allowed within a mile of the place. But on the other hand, as the parent of a missing child, I had every right to be part of any appeal. So this rather uncomfortable compromise had been set.

As for me, I just didn't care. I simply wanted my Anna back.

Sullivan kicked it off, reading from a sheet of paper in front of him and going through the details of Su A's bus journey step-by-step, giving the precise times that the 162 was in the Bromley, Bickley and Chislehurst areas, signing off with the standard line about contacting the police with information that could be of assistance etc.

He then fielded a few questions – none of which were particularly insightful or difficult to answer – before picking up a second piece of paper, clearing his throat and saying: 'Now, moving on … Significant new evidence has come to light connecting this case with the disappearance of Anna Andrews, and we now believe she is being held by the same person, or persons, who are holding Su A Kim.'

I could only presume that the 'significant new evidence' he referred to was the threatening letter that was pushed through my letterbox. Calling it 'significant' was fair enough and it certainly could be described as 'evidence'. But the term 'come to light' somehow suggested it was the fruit of detective work – which it certainly was not. Now perhaps I was being picky, but I couldn't help feeling that certain aspects of this conference were as much to do with PR as detection.

Sullivan then went over a few more details and fielded a few more questions, before a journalist, about two rows back, came up with: 'Is it true that the idea of looking at the bus footage came from Anna and not the police?'

I couldn't actually see Sullivan's face because he was right next to me, but I would imagine that he didn't look too happy.

'We've been studying CCTV footage since the very beginning of this case,' he replied, before the journalist hit back with: 'Yes, but I'm talking about the material from the bus in the opposite direction …'

It was McCullough who answered this: 'Look, we're all working together on this now – and as my colleague has just stated, we're also making significant progress.'

Was this the subtlest of digs at Sullivan? McCullough's use of the word 'now' ('We're all working together *now*') suggested 'we' once weren't.

Had there been a bit of a battle between Sullivan and McCullough relating, amongst other things, to my involvement? It certainly sounded like it.

Then came my part. The part where I had to address the camera directly. God, I'd seen it done a hundred times before: desperate mothers, hopeless pleas.

I'd given this a lot of thought, even writing down a few notes.

In the end I didn't bother with any of it. Didn't need to. I just asked, pleaded, for anyone who knew anything about anything to contact the police – just managing to hold back the tears.

Perhaps knowing that he was watching was what saw me through. I'm no psychologist but I felt that once he knew he'd won, he'd finish with her. To him, it was a game – a game he was winning. And I couldn't afford to let him think he'd won.

THIRTY-ONE

THAT NIGHT, LIZ stayed over. We cooked together, ate together, cleared up together and all the time talked together – about anything except the Anna situation. We shared memories of holidays and long summers, schooldays and old friends, Christmases and families. We even laughed from time to time. But of course the terrible reality was always there, lying in wait.

Sometimes I'd ask her if she thought I should be doing more. Perhaps I should ring round Anna's friends, or drive around putting missing person notices up. But Liz just told me to rest, that the police probably had more information than even I knew about. I went along with this, but didn't really believe it. And as for the appeal, all that had thrown up was a couple of people who said that they might have seen a Korean girl in the area that Saturday, but she was with an older man, a younger woman and a little girl. Hardly abductor material. Another person thought it may just have been a family with a nanny.

But Liz's main words of comfort weren't based on such details – just the ones she'd always used, telling me everything would work out in the end. And thinking back, she'd generally been right – things had tended to work out OK. Please God, make her right this time too.

Eventually, very late, we went to bed. But I didn't really sleep. Just thought and thought and thought.

The next morning, if you can call it the next morning, tired and tearful, I got up – well before the world had started to wake.

I went downstairs, made myself a tea and just sat there, in the living room, thinking.

At times, coming like spasms, I nearly broke down completely. But I didn't quite. Feeling sorry for myself wasn't an option. Feeling sorry for Anna was. If I was going to cry it had to be for her, not for me. Eventually, perhaps an hour later, Liz came down. I'm not sure of the exact time but it was probably about seven. She sat next to me, hugged me and then, finally, I cried.

It's funny, but we'd never been desperately close. Perhaps that was my fault. Yes, there was almost six years between us, but that wasn't it. I suppose, deep down, I'd always been a little jealous of her. She was the slightly taller one, the one with the straighter hair, the more defined features – even the higher grades at school. She'd captured the spirit of the time – flowing and hippy and bright – in a way that I never could.

But now, for perhaps the first time in my life, I really, really needed her.

I left Liz in the lounge, went upstairs, showered and dressed. An hour later we had some breakfast together, though I wasn't really hungry. Next, keeping me busy, she suggested that we should do a supermarket shop. She was right. Not about the food shopping – there was plenty of food in the house – but the keeping busy.

This was perhaps the first day I'd had no real contribution to make. Much as McCullough wanted to keep me involved, he was restricted. I wouldn't, for instance, be involved in today's interrogations of either Christopher or Churchy – neither of whose alibis tied up. Nor would I be talking to Taplow. His claim to have told me about his speaking Korean (of which I still couldn't recall) changed nothing. The point is, he could. Then there was the living in Chislehurst thing, and the coincidental timing of our date. He had much to explain, but I wouldn't be listening in. My participation was coming to an end. Very soon, it would be a case of me moping around the house with nothing more than guilt and regret for company. Plus the occasional jolt of sheer terror and/or expectation at every ring of the phone.

Driving to the supermarket, finding a parking space, getting a trolley, the world seemed a slower, more somnolent place. In the shop, people would recognize me – nudging each other, whispering. At least, I think they were. And everything – the taking things off the shelves; the checking stuff out; the loading the car; the driving home – seemed dreamlike. I was pleased Liz was with me, though. I couldn't have done it without her.

I felt so tired that once we were unpacked, I decided to go back to bed. I told Liz she could go – must go. I kissed her goodbye, told her I really didn't mind being alone. There was only so much she could do. Anyway, she must have been tired herself. She had her own family to get back to. Her youngest was just back from uni and her husband, Pete, wasn't well. She had worries of her own.

Yet again, I was awoken by my bedside phone. I hadn't even realized I'd been sleeping. Turning on my pillow, groping for it and knocking it off its hook – half expecting to have cut the caller off – I put it to my ear.

'Hello.'

'Oh, er, hello, Oh, I hope I didn't wake you....'

'Oh, er, no ... no, it's OK.'

'I don't know if you remember me. It's Mrs Baimbridge ...'

'Yes, of course I do. How are you, Mrs Baimbridge?'

'Oh, mustn't grumble; getting by, I suppose. I'm really sorry to hear about your daughter. I know what you must be going through.'

'Yes, of course,' I said. And she was right. She was one of the few people, the few very people, who really *did* know.

'I didn't know whether to bother you. I'm probably making something out of nothing. But you did say to ring you if I remembered anything. And I've been thinking about it for a while and then I saw you on the television with that terrible business and ...'

'Yes, go on.'

'Well, when they showed where that Korean girl got off the bus and it made me think – you know, that I really should call – because it sort of tied in with ...'

'Tied in with your daughter?'

'Yes. You see, you said you didn't think Rachel had gone to the Imperial War Museum and that she more likely took a train from London Bridge.'

'Yes, that's right.'

'Well, you see, I think she could have taken a train to Chislehurst.'

'Why do you say that?'

'Well, we'd been talking on the phone only a few days before, and she said she was doing this thing for her studies, about the war – you know, families in air raid shelters and stuff. Well, I don't really remember the war myself, I was just a child, but Mum and Dad did, and that's where Mum stayed.'

'Where she stayed?'

'Chislehurst ... Chislehurst Caves.'

'She lived in Chislehurst Caves?'

'Yes, thousands of people did. And now they've got a sort of exhibition there – well, apparently – and anyway, when Rachel said she was going to the War Museum we got talking about the Blitz and things and I happened to mention it.'

'And you suggested she went to Chislehurst Caves?'

'No, no. She was definitely planning to go to the War Museum – the caves thing just came up in conversation.'

'And you only just remembered this?'

'Yes, I got thinking after you left about what she could have done. You see, Chislehurst is on the same train route as Orpington and she was supposed to be coming home that weekend – so it would make more sense than going off to the War Museum – and maybe she realized that.'

'Yes, maybe.'

'And then I saw the thing on television about the Korean girl on the bus and they mentioned she got off at Chislehurst, so, as I said, it sort of tied in.'

After repeating her sympathies towards me, I thanked her for calling, we said goodbye and I put the phone back down. I then hitched myself up on the pillow and thought about what she'd said.

It certainly was a lead, but it was a tenuous one. The only connection that Su A's disappearance had with Chislehurst Caves was: a) she got off at the High Street – a mile up the road from the caves. And b) the mother of Rachel Baimbridge – a girl who had disappeared some ten years earlier in an entirely unrelated case – *might* have mentioned the caves a few days before her disappearance. So should I ring McCullough with such flimsy stuff?

After readjusting the pillow and making myself more comfortable, I thought about it and decided yes, I should. After all, if Mrs Baimbridge was prepared to take the trouble to ring me, the least I could do was forward her thoughts to the police – the poor woman deserved that. And anyway, I needed to ring McCullough about another sudden thought I'd had. On the note, did the words 'Got your daughter' and 'Check DNA on this' suggest, yet again, that it was written by a non-native speaker? Shouldn't it read 'I've got your daughter' and 'Check *the* DNA on this'? Or could it yet again be a case someone trying to deceive us into thinking they're a foreign speaker? On the other hand, maybe I was just obsessing about it all too much; after all, in note form, we often leave words out. Anyway, I decided it was worth a call. Any new thoughts were.

I didn't have his number stored on my landline, so I got up, went to the dressing table, picked up my mobile (briefly catching my reflection in the mirror – truly awful), took it back to bed, selected his number and hit it. All I got back was an engaged tone. So I hung up, and put it down by my bedside phone.

Then I started thinking about Chislehurst Caves again. You

see, I had this sort of inherited memory of them. I say inherited because I'd never actually been there.

When I was young, I wanted to do the things my big sister did. For years I had this idealized mental picture – a sort of distant yearning. Because Liz went to all these gigs there – witnessed many of the greats there: Hendrix, the Stones, Bowie, in what I imagined as some kind of subterranean nirvana – and I didn't. Not that it was the bands; it wasn't. I just wanted to be part of the happening – the crazy clothes, the boys, the mixing with the types of people my parents disapproved of.

And that, still, was the mental picture I got from those two words: Chislehurst Caves.

I got up, went downstairs to the lounge, drew the curtains – no journalists – sat down with my laptop and Googled it. Ostensibly, I was checking if there could possibly be any link to the Su A case, but in truth I suppose it was all just a merciful diversion.

The official site – 'Chislehurst Caves: Miles of History Below Your Feet'– was suitably dark and ominous. However, it did feature a smiling cartoon bat, flapping away merrily next to details of opening times and guided tours etc. These were given as being seven days a week, on the hour, between 10 a.m. till 4 p.m. It also said there was no need to pre-book. Below this was a YouTube clip. I pressed the play button and up came a few silent seconds of hand-held camera work – dark tunnels, spooky waxworks and stone carvings of skeletons and hobgoblins – all apparently lit by oil lamps. Having played this, up popped another half-dozen clips, arranged in a row along the bottom of the webpage. I clicked onto the first one and up came some rather amateur footage of one of the tours. A tour guide was talking to a group of visitors and I could just about pick up what she was saying – that the tour would cover just one mile of the full twenty-two. This amazed me. I mean, I obviously realized there were some pretty big caverns down there, otherwise you couldn't have had concerts. But I hadn't realized it was that big.

The clip finished, so I clicked the next one. It was a section of a TV documentary called *Most Haunted*, which, as its name suggested, dealt with the most haunted places in Britain – of which the caves, apparently, was one. The material looked terrifying in itself. A woman reporter, filmed with a night-vision camera – ashen face and illuminated eyes – was breathlessly telling us of the ghouls, phantoms and poltergeists that apparently inhabit the place.

Clearly, they were trying to scare the pants off people – and in my case, pretty much succeeding.

With absolutely nothing else on that day – based on Mrs Baimbridge's call and its proximity to the 162 bus route – I decided the caves were perhaps worth a visit.

I suppose I was also interested in laying the ghost of some very old non-memories too.

THIRTY-TWO

DECEMBER 21ST. SHORTEST day. Weather cold. Sky grey and light fading.

Driving to the caves, the big Bickley residences – mostly unlit for Christmas, way too posh for that – loomed up to the left and right, faded by, and disappeared into the darkness behind me. At one stage, a car seemed to be on my tail. But the next time I looked, the road was empty again.

Dropping steeply, I slowed right down to look for directions to the caves. I knew they were at the bottom of the valley – and somewhere off to the right – but in the gloom I couldn't see the signpost.

Driving slowly on, I found a row of shops. I was pretty sure they were walkable from here, so I pulled over and stopped. In my rear-view mirror, some fifty metres back, another vehicle did the same.

I was on the verge of getting out to ask for directions when I saw the sign – just ahead and, as I'd expected, off to the right. I re-indicated, pulled back out and threw a right. The other car didn't appear to move.

Just a few metres on, I found the car park. I drove in, switched off, and got out. All but empty. Most families, I suppose, had opted for last-minute food shopping or browsing for stocking fillers, rather than traipsing around gloomy tunnels. I can't say I blamed them. Oh yes, and no cars seemed to follow me in.

I'd half expected to find an ominously black cavern-shaped hole awaiting me, but according to the sign, the entrance to the cave was via nothing scarier than a pleasant, pavilion-style building – complete with veranda, and alfresco tables and chairs, all of which, unsurprisingly, were unoccupied at this time of year.

I pushed through the swing doors and found myself in an area not dissimilar to a motorway service area, though its décor was slightly more log-cabin-like. About a half-dozen people were standing around looking at postcards, buying knick-knacks and, presumably, waiting for the next tour to start. I bought a ticket from the combined ticket office/gift shop and browsed the souvenirs – most of which tended towards the war years (replica posters, Glenn Miller CDs), archaeology (fossils, ammonites) and horror movies (fake spiders, plastic vampire bats etc). Not wishing to invite recognition, I kept well away from the other visitors. Whether judgemental or sympathetic, I was growing fed up with the nudges and the stares.

After a few minutes, despite there being so few people, a vague queue began to form in a roped-off area that led to the double doors at the back of the room. I looked at my watch. It was 3.58.

I joined the back of the queue and noted that even before entering the caves proper, an area had been cordoned off to accommodate a small display of First and Second World War memorabilia: ARP helmets, ration books and gas masks etc. Mrs Baimbridge was right. It was an obvious place to do some field-work on Second World War family life.

A large bearded man, clearly our guide for the day, walked to the front of the queue. He bid us a good afternoon, introduced himself as Will, and asked us to follow him.

When I got through the double doors, my first impressions were far from favourable – just a featureless concrete passageway, complete with neon lights and iron handrails. Frankly, we could easily have been entering an inner-city pedestrian subway.

We walked for a few minutes, going ever downwards, getting

ever colder, until we reached a point where concrete walls gave out to rough-hewn chalk. Then Will stopped. At his feet, a cluster of hurricane lamps flickered. Ahead of us lay total blackness.

We formed a small huddle around him, with me at the back. He said that we wouldn't all need a lamp – about one for every third person would be more than sufficient. Fine by me; I was happy with the anonymity that darkness gave.

After a short walk, illuminated only by our lanterns, we came to a small cavern. On its facing wall was a map of the caves and, pointing at the map, Will told us that the caves could be divided into three areas – Druid, Saxon and Roman.

Druids? Saxons? Wasn't that what Albert Christopher was so into? There again, Farrell gave lectures on all that mythical, magical stuff too.

I looked back up at the map, comparing the section we'd already walked through to the network that was still ahead of us. Its sheer size became immediately apparent. Effectively, an underground town.

Could someone really be held down here undetected for months on end? Studying the network more carefully, I found myself believing they could. After all, if girls could be incarcerated in suburban basements for years on end – cases of which had been recently uncovered in both America and Austria – then surely they could be hidden in twenty-two miles of pitch-black, uninhabited tunnelling. I made up my mind, there and then. Once this tour was finished, I'd be asking this Will a few extra questions of my own.

After running through their violent past, full of murders and mayhem, then scaring us witless with stories of ghouls and ghosts – which he claimed to encounter on an almost daily basis – he led us forward.

Walking behind the lamp-lit group, I noted the maze becoming ever more complex, with every darkened tunnel having further tunnels leading off it. Most of those passageways, when you peered down them, seemed to spawn further tunnels – some running off at right angles, some forking into two, and some descending ever deeper. I also noted passageways blocked to the ceiling with fallen rubble and others seeming to offer vague, distant luminance. But mostly they were just impenetrably black. Portals into nothingness.

Every so often we'd come across one of the exhibits. A stage, fitted out with drum kit and amplifiers, where Hendrix and Bowie performed – and from where Radio Caroline, the pirate radio station, used to run its 1960s Caves Club. Then an underground hospital, where Cavena (yes, that was her actual name), the only war baby ever born down there, was being tended to by waxwork doctors and nurses. And a subterranean church, complete with candles, pews, altar and even dummy parishioners.

'They had everything they needed,' said Will, pointing out toilets and washing facilities as we passed them by. 'And don't forget, although it seems a little chilly down here, the temperature never gets colder than it is now – a permanent ten degrees Celsius, summer or winter – unless you have lots of people down here, when it warms up rapidly. In fact, during the war they had the opposite problem – it became unbearably hot.'

At one point, we arrived at an underground pool. Will paused, turned, and beckoned us to the water's edge. Once we were gathered together, he held his lamp aloft and, peering down at the water, said: 'This is the Haunted Pool. Over two hundred years ago a violent murder was committed here. The victim was eventually found at the bottom of the water – her body weighted down with stones.' He then paused, turning his sights towards the cavern entrance: 'To this day, a ghostly apparition can be seen walking these tunnels – I've seen her myself.'

There were a couple of giggling girls at the front of the group, one of whom asked: 'What does she look like?'

Will stooped to her and whispered: 'About your height, pale and sad looking.'

'And what is she wearing?' asked her friend.

'A long white dress,' replied Will. 'And a shawl around her shoulders and bonnet on her head.'

He then put his lantern down by the poolside, pulled himself back up to his full height, breathed in deeply and suddenly boomed out 'Aaaaaaaargh' at the very top of his voice.

Of course, we all nearly jumped out of our skins – especially the two girls standing next to him.

He then smiled and said: 'Sorry about that. I do hope I didn't scare you. But now I have a question. Did you hear anything after I shouted, and can you hear anything now?'

We all stood in silence until a man at the front plucked up the courage to respond: 'Er, no, I don't think I heard anything else at all.'

'Precisely,' said Will. 'That's because this is the only part of the entire caves with absolutely no echo. You see, the echo died with the woman.'

'Do it again,' asked one of the girls, clearly gaining in courage.

'OK,' he said – and he did. He was right. No echo.

'And I'll do it a third time too – in another part of the caves – just to show you what I mean about the echo.'

Our little group now suitably impressed, he then went on to tell us that this was also the only part of the cave complex that remained unoccupied during the war. 'You see, no one would sleep here. In fact, during the 1950s, there was something called the Chislehurst Challenge. Anyone who would sleep here overnight would be offered the princely sum of £5 – a large sum in those days.'

'Did anyone do it?' asked one of the girls.

'Only one,' he said. 'But the poor soul knocked himself unconscious trying to escape. They found him the next morning. He was alive, but completely insane. Since then the practice has been banned. No one is now allowed to stay down here overnight.' He then moved a step closer and asked: 'Fancy a bit of shut-eye?'

We all shook our heads and edged away.

You know, I didn't, and still don't, believe in all this paranormal stuff. But it did offer a pleasant – or perhaps unpleasant – distraction from the real world, and I was perhaps able to forget myself for a few minutes. Anything was better than reality.

During the next section – a particularly long, straight tunnel – Will told us that there were nine Druids altars in this part of the caves.

'They used them for blood sacrifices,' he said.

On hearing this, the two girls – now sticking to Will like glue – made the mistake of asking him what was sacrificed. 'Young girls, of course,' he said bluntly.

Continuing on, we came to a small, semi-circular cavern, to the back of which was a large ledge – almost like a stage. We edged forward, and stopped right in front of it.

'This,' said Will, drawing his hurricane lamp to his face, 'is where humans were sacrificed. On this very altar girls would lie, face down, with their heads above this ridge.'

He then looked down towards a carved-out notch at the front of the ledge. 'The priest would then slice her throat open with a shard of razor-sharp flint – knapped from these very caves.'

Then, switching rapidly from the sublime to the ridiculous, he rather matter-of-factly informed us that the word knapsack came from the sacks that knappers would sling over their shoulder with their flint in it. He then switched rapidly back to ghoul-mode, telling us that the girl's blood would run down into the notch where it was collected in ceremonial vessels.

'What did they do with the blood?' asked one of the girls.

'Drank it,' replied Will. 'While it was still warm.'

The girls pulled yucky faces and giggled.

'Now,' said Will, 'Back to the echo. Let's try it again. Only this time, if I may, I'll take your lamps.'

He told us that he was going to walk around the corner to another cave and leave us, without our lanterns, in total darkness. He said that if any of us were scared of the dark, the real dark, we'd be welcome to follow him. We all agreed to stay where we were.

Being a small group, we only had four lanterns between us and, walking solemnly back past us, he took them one-by-one. He then continued to walk, lamps in hand, back down the dark passageway.

We all watched him walk away – the orange light slowly diminishing, until he took a distant left – leaving only a weakest of orange hues behind him. This in turn disappeared and we were left in blackness. Absolute nothingness.

In the illuminated world in which we live, eyes-wide-open blackness is something we seldom experience. This was. And it is claustrophobic in the extreme – almost suffocating. In fact, after about a minute, it really began to get to me. Normally, I wouldn't say I was scared by the dark, but in that void it felt as if I was no longer in control.

I started thinking. If you were incarcerated down here, and if your captor was the owner of the only light source, he would have total power. Down here, light would be as valuable as food, water and air.

Suddenly, there was a huge boom – its echo going on and on and on. Clearly this wasn't Will's voice – more likely some kind of drum or metal tank. But it made Will's point perfectly, especially in the dark. The echo was back.

He soon came back to us, with lanterns in hand, whistling happily as he drew nearer. Once he'd reached us, he cracked a joke about whistling in the dark, handed us our lamps back, and asked us to follow him once more.

After the Druid's Cavern, there was little else to see apart from more passageways, tunnels and caves, and eventually we found our way back to the original WWII entry cubicle, where the tour had started.

This booth – omitted from his opening talk – was little more than an underground hut built into the bare rock face. Through its windows you could see a mock-up of how it must have been back in the 1940s – a dim bulb lighting a lifeless dummy of a ticket collector as he sat at his desk – his rubber stamp held aloft, forever frozen in time.

Will said goodbye to us, we thanked him, and started to amble our way to the exit – though I hung back a little.

'I'm sorry to bother you, Will, but I wonder if I could ask you a question or two.'

'Fire away,' he said.

'Well, I was wondering if just anybody is allowed to come down here. You know, unaccompanied.'

'No,' he replied, shaking his head. 'Not at all. These caves are privately owned. Only people working here can come down.'

'And are there any parts that even you never go to?'

'Sure,' he said. 'The vast majority. Most of it is all the same – just tunnel after tunnel.'

'Would anybody go there, to these other parts?'

'Why would they? There's nothing much there.'

'And if somebody did get in – somebody who didn't actually work here – and they went to these other parts of the cave, would you know about it?

'Me?'

'Well, no, not just you – anybody. Would it be obvious someone was down here?'

'Well, I suppose we'd probably hear noises – even if they were a long way away. You heard that echo, didn't you?'

I thought for a second: 'Have you heard any noises – you know, not from the general public or anything?'

'Of course, all the time – the caves are haunted.'

Stupid question. I just pressed on: 'Have you seen anybody down here? You know, people that maybe shouldn't be?'

He was beginning to look at me a little suspiciously. Even though it was dark, did he perhaps recognisz me?

'No,' he finally answered. 'I can't see how anybody would get in without being noticed. It's all locked up at night.'

'And is this the only entrance?'

'Oh no,' he said. 'There's Labyrinthe's entrance for a start,' and with a slightly wearisome look, added: 'That's the original Roman opening. Labyrinthe is a role-play club, Dungeons and Dragons, that sort of thing.' Clearly role-plays weren't his thing.

'And nowhere else?'

'Officially, no,' he said, 'but there's also the Cavaliers Passage. That comes down from someone's back garden somewhere in Chislehurst. I think it's blocked up now though.'

Someone's back garden in Chislehurst? Taplow's maybe?

'And that's it?' I asked. 'Just those three places?'

'Well, there's supposed to be a number of deneholes.'

'Deneholes?'

'Yes, they're shafts cut into the chalk – there are quite a few in this part of Kent.'

He then shrugged and added: 'No one knows exactly what they were for, possibly to excavate the chalk, for agriculture. They're supposed to date back to Saxon times.'

'Are they very accessible?'

'Not really. Most of them are lost in the woods – covered and forgotten. But I suppose, well, if you can find them … then maybe….' He then thought for a second. 'But anyway, even if you found one and unblocked it, it would be very dangerous. Most of them are just vertical drops into the caves. You'd almost need climbing gear.'

'But not all of them?'

'Well, I've heard it said that some are no more than holes in the ground you can drop into – but I've never found one.'

I had this sudden thought: *Holes in the ground you can drop into?* Like a tomb. Like a mudum.

'And you could get to the caves through them?'

'Yes, I suppose so, if you could find one – and knew what you were doing.'

'Look, Will, I, er, hope you don't mind my calling you Will?'

'No, er …'

'My name's Pam, by the way.'

'Oh, er … Hi, Pam.'

We exchanged a slightly awkward handshake – his hands being surprisingly gentle.

'Erm, if I mention some names, could you say if you've heard of any of them – if any of them are connected to these caves?'

'Sorry?' he said, his suspicion mounting. 'I'm not sure I can –'

'Look,' I interrupted, 'if you haven't guessed who I am by now, I'll tell you – I'm that woman you might have seen on the news. I'm desperate to find my daughter, so if you could just answer a straight yes or no.'

He looked at me thoughtfully, but didn't reply, so I just pressed on.

'Does the name Paul Farrell mean anything to you?'

'No, never heard of him.'

'How about Edward Taplow?

'No … er, look, Pam, I really don't think I can give you this information, I mean …'

He turned and started to walk towards the exit.

With only a spooky waxwork of a wartime ticket collector for company, I called out one last time: 'Look, Will, I really, really need your help on this …How about Albert Christopher?'

He paused and turned. 'Albert?' he said brightly. 'Yes, of course, nice bloke, used to be one of the guides here – still comes down here from time to time – knows this place like the back of his …' Will's voice trailed away, the brief cheer in his face dropping.

Mr Smiling-and-Helpful. Mr Middle-Aged Family Man. Albert Joseph Christopher.

THIRTY-THREE

HURRYING FROM CAVE-black to car-park-dark, my first thought was to make that call to McCullough. What had once been a vague hunch was now a strong likelihood. Christopher needed finding, the caves needed searching, and both now.

Maybe that was the problem. Maybe that was why, as I hurried along, juggling mobile phone and car keys, I didn't notice that the hazard warning lights didn't flash when I zapped my car.

Then I slid into the driver's seat, mobile to ear, and …

I can't breathe, can't move. Choking, asphyxiating, my neck clamped from behind. Tightening and tightening. I put my hand to my throat; it makes no difference. Tighter and tighter. Windpipe compressed. Respiratory system closing down. I start to black out.

I come round. Grip loosened. Gasping. Breathing.

Punches. To my face, to my head. Pain. Slam, slam. Stabbing pain. Dull, deep pain. Body screaming. Ears screaming. More punches. Blood. Nose. Mouth. Face.

I'm gagged. Hands tied; cutting into my wrists. I'm dragged. Can't scream. Can't breathe. Pushed, kicked. Dumped into back seat. Door slams.

Car starts moving.

Face down. Back seat. Knees on floor, face into seat. Still can't breathe. Blood from nose. From everywhere. Warm pool forming around my face. I can feel it, smell it, taste it.

We drive. Up through gears, but then back down a gear. Uphill, I think. We level off. Drive for a couple of minutes. Now slowing; turning, probably. Driving slowly. Bumpy road. Uneven road. We stop. Ignition off. Doors opens.

Pulling me out. My arm, my hair. More pain. Dragged. Fall. Hit ground. Face first. Smell earth. Taste dirt.

'Get up!' he shouts.

I don't move. Can't move.

Ribs kicked. Pain shoots through. Winded, stabbed with pain. Can't breathe. Can't catch my breath.

'Get up.'

I start to think. Why resist? I don't care about pain. I care about Anna. Seeing her one last time. That's why I'm here, isn't it? Why refuse now? What's the point of dying here? Do as he says; he'll take me to Anna.

Using the car as leverage, I try to haul myself up. But with hands tied behind my back, I can't.

He helps me up. Sees I'm beaten. I've surrendered now. So he helps me.

On my feet, but hunched. He's in front of me. He switches on a torch, straight in my face. Dazzling. I flinch, turn away. Purple circles swim in front of me.

The light leaves my face. I open my eyes. Look at him.

Even in a balaclava, the eyes and nose are enough. Gone is the woolly tanktop, gone are the comfy corduroys. Head-to-toe army fatigues. It is indeed Christopher.

He turns the torch up to his own face. Just like the guide in the caves. Strangely, it's laughable, childish.

'Well done, bitch. You finally did it. You got me. Trouble is I got you first.'

Somehow, I no longer care. I don't know why, but I'm released. From fear, from pain. Even from the fear of pain. A strange epiphany.

My nose feels broken, my ribs ache and I've spat teeth out.

Face and arms cut, dirt and grit in wounds. I've even peed myself. But nothing matters. Nothing hurts. I just want to see Anna. Maybe he'll accept me instead of her. I'd take that. That would be a bargain.

We are at the end of a long, unmade road. No houses, no lights. Just black trees on both sides. And beyond the black trees, I couldn't say. Maybe more trees.

He grabs my shoulders, turns me. Now I'm facing the end of the road. A dense, black wood. And a gate, I think. Yes, a gate. He pushes me forward.

We walk. Well, he walks, I limp. Through the gate – his torch behind me – illuminating my path. We continue. I stumble, falter, but walk again. He keeps pushing me, prodding me, kicking me.

Twigs and branches, caught in the torchlight, look surprisingly beautiful. How strange.

Thorns and brambles attack my face from both sides, but they're OK too. They don't hurt. I didn't expect it to be like this. I thought the end would be more dreadful, more painful.

The deeper we go, the more impossible it becomes. Even with him prodding at me, I keep going wrong. He curses me, takes the lead – pulling me by my coat.

We stop. I can see no difference here. It all looks the same.

He lets go of me, leaves me, moving a few steps forward.

He's stooping, kicking leaves, his torchlight searching the ground.

He puts his torch down on the forest floor, carefully directing the beam towards me. It's supposed to be illuminating me. But it isn't. Just the dead leaves.

I suppose, for the first time, I could try to run away – or stumble away, at least. But what would be the point?

No more than a black shadow, he bends to the ground. He's pulling a slab – the grating hollowness telling me it's stone. He stands up again, smacking his hands together, brushing off the dirt.

'Over here,' he says.

I do as I'm told. Hobble forward.

Looking down, a dark shape. Oblong. He picks up the torch. A hole. Like a grave. This would be where poor Su A made her final call. Her mudum.

I start thinking about this, the detective in me, thinking, right to the end. If she still had her mobile on her, it must have been because she didn't know – hadn't realized – till this point. So unlike me, she must have been a willing passenger in his car. Probably only started to resist as he told her to go into the dense woods. Then got absolutely desperate and tried to make the call, as he pushed her down this hole.

Like I said, the detective in me, right to the end, still working things out.

With his torch-beam darting around its sides, I step to its edge. In front of me, blackness. I've no way of knowing how deep it is, but logically, it shouldn't be. Still thinking. Still working things out.

I step into the nothingness, hit the bottom. Almost no time between jump and impact. I was right. But with hands tied and mouth gagged, I still crash; gash myself again.

Lying crumpled, I can taste the earth, taste the blood.

A thump, inches from my face, shaking the ground and throwing up dirt. His boots. He's jumped too.

'Up,' he says, shining his torch in my face.

Again, I can't do it by myself. He helps me up, linking arms under mine.

I'm standing, stooped. He releases me and directs the torch to the pit's floor – the beam moving around its edges. He stops. He's found a second darkness. No reflected light. Just a black hole. He plays the beam around its edges. It's perhaps three feet in diameter.

'Go,' he gestures.

I stoop down, as if to go headfirst.

'No,' he says, grabbing me by the hair and kicking my feet forward. 'Feet first.'

So I sit back down again, painfully, bumping to the floor. With hands tied behind my back, it's difficult to sit upright. He helps me, hauling me up into a sitting position.

'Feet in,' he says.

I shuffle my bottom forwards, dangling my feet into the well. It doesn't feel sheer – perhaps forty-five degrees.

He knees my back. I shuffle further forward. He kicks me again: 'Go.'

I do what he says, half-falling, half-scrabbling, sliding downwards, using my feet as a brake. Within a few seconds I hit another floor. Again, I find myself in a crumpled heap.

A thud hits my back. His boots, hitting me. He can't get through, I'm blocking the passageway. He's kicking at me, cursing.

I roll forward, out of his way.

A second or two passes. His torch light is on my face.

'Up,' he says.

Again, I can't do it by myself. So he helps me up – but I'm getting a little better at it, using the cave's wall as leverage.

It's totally black, but this cave feels bigger. Maybe the coolness, maybe the echo, but bigger. He points the torch: 'That way.'

We walk forward, his torch behind me, casting my shadow on the walls. I don't know how far we're going, but it's slow. I'm almost crippled, gagged and gasping. I have to keep stopping.

Hobbling forward, every tunnel is becoming the same. On and on. The walls, caught in his torchlight, are of dirty chalk; the ground uneven. I could be just five feet from where Will took us on that tour, or five miles. Down here, you'd never know.

Way ahead, I couldn't say how far, I think I can see a slight amberness. Very, very slight. We stop. He shines his light into the distance. I can no longer see anything particularly different, but perhaps he can. We walk on.

Yes, as I jolt forward, I'm sure there's an orangeness. It's definitely a light of some kind.

The nearer we get, the more obvious it is. It has a slight glimmer, a flicker. Nearer and nearer.

Now I can see an outline of a cavern. As much as is possible in my condition, I quicken my pace. Somehow, I just know I need to be in that place. Even if it's the last place I ever see.

He pushes me forward. I take two steps.

THIRTY-FOUR

STRANGE. I SHOULDN'T be thinking this but it's beautiful, almost. Yet only lamps – the same the visitors use. Golden warmth, flickering, magical, even.

The lanterns circle the base of the walls. Apart from on one side. At that point, the line of lights seem to cut straight across the stone floor, isolating the far section of the cave into darkness.

I limp forward a little, drawn to that dark area. Now I can see why that section remains in darkness.

There's a raised slab, like a step, about two feet higher than the rest of the cave floor. The hurricane lamps are placed along the foot of it, so the raised area that goes back to the far wall remains unlit. Did I say raised area? It's not just a raised area. It's an altar.

I hobble forward. There's something on the altar. A pile of blankets.

'Go on,' says Christopher, his voice echoing. 'It's what you've been looking for.'

I look down. There's a step cut into the front of the altar. But it's not a step. It's cut out for a particular purpose. I know what that's for too – and shudder at the thought.

Slowly, painfully, I haul myself up onto the slab. I take another step forward. Yes, blankets, a quilt, an old bedspread.

The rags stir, move slightly. Whoever it is – whatever it is – is alive. *'It's what you've been looking for.'* Surely Anna? But he could mean Su A.

I have mixed feelings. Anna, reduced to this existence, is

horrible. But at least it's an existence. At least she's still alive. Whoever's missing, Anna or Su A, probably isn't.

It moves again. Whoever it is is waking up. Let it be Anna.

From within, the quilt is slowly being nudged down. Black hair; straight black hair. Flat, brown forehead. Oval eyes. It's not Anna.

Su A's eyes look up at me, unblinking. Suddenly, hate – her eyes screwing up, her nostrils flaring. Rage, fury. She shouts words at me, curses, screams.

From behind me, Christopher mumbles something. In Korean, I think. She calms, stops.

'Surprised?' says Christopher. 'Shocked that your little Korean girl doesn't really want you after all? That's where you fucking do-gooders get it wrong. She's even beginning to like me now, aren't you, Su?'

He then darts the beam to an area at the back of the cave: 'Even gets pride of place in our little camp now. Look, that's where she used to be.'

I peer into the area his torch has found. Up against the cavern wall is another pile of blankets. He turns his torch back away from it, leaving it in total blackness.

I move towards it, stumbling, drawn to the dark.

Little more than rags – a heap – from which two rusty chains snake their way across the rock floor.

It moves a little. This time it must be Anna. Has to be.

I move a little closer, try to speak her name. But through my gag it just comes out muffled. The pile struggles, trying to get out. Hands must be tied, like me. I drop to my knees, bury my face in it.

Using my nose, my chin, my face, I pull at the rags. Even try using my teeth through the gagging.

The struggling stops. It's as if she knows. Slowly, inch by inch, I ease the cloth down. Even in this darkness, I recognize the first few strands of her hair. It's Anna.

Forehead, eyes – beautiful, terrified eyes – then face. She's gagged, but doesn't look damaged – not cut or bruised, or beaten. Thank God.

I look into her eyes. A million emotions are there: helplessness; hopelessness; fear and love. But the one word her eyes say, the one word I just won't accept, is sorry. Sorry for what, Anna? I'm the one who should be saying sorry. I try to convey this through my own eyes.

I lean forward. We touch. Nose to nose. Cheek to cheek. Gagged-mouth to gagged-mouth. And the miracle is, despite the filth, despite the squalor, she still smells of Anna. My lovely Anna.

I pull back a little. She has tears in her eyes. I don't want that. No, you mustn't cry, Anna.

'OK,' says Christopher, shining his torch on us. 'Enough. Enough mother-on-daughter action,' he laughs.

He grabs me, pulls me off her, kicks me. I can't shield myself – he just kicks and kicks, shoves me across the stone slab.

I open my eyes, Christopher still standing over me. He moves his beam down my body, finds another rusty chain, bends down; fastens it to my ankle.

He steps back, takes off his balaclava, pauses, laughs. He gets down off the altar and bends down to the nearest lantern. He lifts it up and turns it out.

One by one, darker and darker, he extinguishes them. We are in almost total darkness. One remaining.

He walks to it, holds it up to his face, and smiles back at us. He then turns and walks. Step by step, the light fades.

Total blackness. Total silence. Total nothing.

Will those be the last moments? The last time I touch her, smell her, see her?

I move a little, try to ease the pain. My chain scrapes on the floor.

I have an idea.

Painfully, I edge to the chain. I pick it up and strike the floor with it. Three clunks: One … two … three.

Will she understand?

I wait for a second, do it again: One … two … three. *I … love … you.*

And then again.

Seconds go by. I hear her move.

Four clunks come back: *I … love … you … too?*

I couldn't say how much time went by. It's impossible to tell. At one stage, I touched my wrist; feeling for my watch. Futile, anyway – I couldn't have seen it. But either way, it was gone. I still learnt something though. You see, I'd never lost it before. Yes, he'd been kicking me, punching me, pushing me. But I was pretty sure he'd removed it on purpose – probably when I was nearly uncon- scious. Why? Because, with or without lamps, he didn't want me knowing how much time had passed. Hours, days, weeks? All part of the softening-up process. All part of the torture.

It was only a tiny point, but that knowledge almost comforted me. I could still read him. Undefeated, right to the end.

More time went by. Maybe hours. Yes, probably hours. I found myself wondering who'd realize first. That I was missing, I mean. My neighbours? No chance. With all the comings and goings recently they wouldn't even question it. McCullough? Again, no. He'd just assume I needed some time, some space – it would be days before he became suspicious. My sister, then? Maybe, but again, it could be a while – ringing at least three or four times before alerting anyone. Possibly the cave tour guide would be first, or someone he'd told the tale to – about the woman on TV who mentioned the man he used to work with. But how long would that take?

I can't say it was sleep. Neither dreaming nor thinking. Just a different form of consciousness, I suppose.

I was a child again. A warm seaside night, walking with Mum and Dad. I'm holding their hands, swinging between them. Along the front, illuminating the gardens, are magic lights of gold and green and blue.

Letting go, I dart away, crouching down and studying them

more closely. Night-time flowerbeds, transformed into little worlds of fairytale and beauty.

Is this them? Are these the visions we've all heard about? The fleeting early-years memories we see right at the end, when death takes us?

Then another memory. This time of Anna. A similar age, but a sunny day. Pedalling her little red car on the pavement – giggling and screeching, racing me to the gate. No dad in this image, though.

I'm not going to let these images suck me in. I need to remain conscious.

Anna was a sticking-plaster baby. That's what they call them, don't they? A baby David and I decided to go for, five years into our rocky marriage, to patch things up – though we never admitted as much. Well, in a way, it worked. Not the patching up; our relationship continued to crumble. But the sticking-plaster bit. She may not have saved our marriage but she saved my life. Without her, I could never have made it.

I'm fully awake. At least, I think I am. I move my hand up to my eyelids. I flutter the back of my hand with my lashes, making sure my eyes are open. They are. Unless, of course that's part of a dream too, which I don't think it is.

Occasionally, I hear a slight noise, a stirring. It could be Su A, it could be Anna. I consider clanking the chains again to keep contact. But decide against it. If Anna's sleeping, it's for the best. The only thing she has.

What's that thing many a parent has said? If I had to choose. My life, for the life of my child? I'd sacrifice mine, every time. Well, for most, it never comes to pass. But for me, in this situation, it just could. And if, at some stage, in this stinking hole, I get the chance to prolong her life at the expense of mine, I'll take it. If he's going to kill us, he can take me first. Even if it only extends her life by minutes, it would be worth it. Who knows, during those minutes, she could still be saved. It would be a chance well worth taking.

Semi-conscious, more time goes by. I couldn't say how long. Maybe a night, maybe days and nights. At one stage I pee myself again. This time it's almost welcoming. Human, warm and wet. I'm close to the end, I think.

A noise. Yes, definitely a noise. Footsteps. Closer, closer.

A light, flitting across the far cave wall. Dim, but brightening. It's a torch. It's him.

In my face. Dazzling. Stinging my eyes, I flinch.

I open my eyes again. Feeling slightly stronger now.

A few seconds pass. He's lighting the lanterns again. One by one. I look over to Anna. She's awake. So is Su A.

I look back at him. He's little more than a silhouette, but he seems to be wearing something … white robes.

He walks further into the cave, gets up onto the altar.

'Hello, girls.'

He walks up to me, kneels down. He's taking off my gag.

Breathing heavily, it's a wonderful relief.

'You can scream if you want,' he says, getting up. 'This place is deserted now.'

I've got no intention of screaming. Wouldn't give him the pleasure.

He walks back across the slab, torch down, away from me, past Anna, past the watching Su A.

I look over to Anna. My lovely Anna. I'd like to tell her not to be scared, not to be frightened – just like I used to when she was a child, woken in the night by some terrible nightmare. But words with scared and frightened in them won't help.

'I love you' is all I say – my whispered words echoing in the cold, still air. 'We'll find a way. I know we will.'

I'm not sure I believe this.

Now I say the thing mothers always say: 'Don't worry.'

How could she not worry? It's ridiculous, but I say it.

'I love you. Don't worry.'

I look back at him. He's left the altar, kneeling down, doing something.

Do I glimpse someone else? Behind him, in the gloom of the cave entrance? A woman, maybe? Could there be someone else down here? Just my imagination, probably.

He gets up, walks over, jumps back onto the altar.

'I must confess,' he says, smiling, holding out his robed arms like some Christ figure. 'I'd like to have made more of this. More of a ceremony, I mean. But, well, time's against us, I'm afraid.'

He seems to be holding something. A branch or twig of some kind. He takes a step nearer.

'Mistletoe,' he says, smiling slightly, letting the realization sink in. 'Do you know where the idea of kissing under this stuff comes from? Fertility. Druids.'

He lifts it further. 'White seed, you see. Male seed – that's why. When everything else is dormant – in mid-winter – this stuff comes to life. White seed. And oh yes, red blood – for death. Semen and blood. Mistletoe and wine. Sort of symmetrical. Kind of perfect. And oh yes, pretty much Winter Solstice too.'

'*Pretty much*', he said. I reckon only a day or so has passed. Ever the detective.

He walks over to Anna, bends over her, grabs her covers, rips them off.

She's naked.

Writhing and struggling – fear, panic in her eyes. He utters some words – not English, not even Korean.

He undoes her leg clamps, pulls her legs apart – kneels between them. Still gagged and bound, she's twisting from side to side. There's nothing she can do. Nothing I can do, except scream, and I'm not going to do that.

He looks upward, uttering more words. He takes some of the white seed, discarding the branches, turning my way and throwing them towards me.

He squeezes the seed between his fingers, leans back over Anna – smears it over her body.

Kneeling back up, he takes something from the robe. It catches the light.

'Blood and seed,' he says.

Sudden realization. It's flint. Razor-sharp flint.

He holds it aloft. 'Blood and seed,' he repeats.

He slowly lowers it. His other hand is under his robe – playing with himself, arousing himself.

More words.

He takes his hand back out and unties her gag.

Screaming, screaming. Piercing, terrible, heartbreaking. Just the sound is killing me.

He picks up the flint, presses it to her neck.

I can't just watch. I have to do something. What did I say to myself? If I get the chance to prolong her life, make the ultimate sacrifice. But what can I use? Screaming and pleading won't help. It'll just turn him on more. He's a psychopath – he loves women in pain. That's why he's taken our masks off – so he can hear us screaming. I need to be cleverer than that. Break through his pleasure barrier. Rile him. Turn him off.

He's crouched over her, flint pressed on her neck – hand back under his robe, slowly stimulating himself.

Yes, break though his pleasure barrier, turn him off. Show him I'm not scared. Women with power. Women in control. That's what he hates.

'Christopher!' I shout.

It has no effect. He just continues rubbing himself, savouring the moment.

'Christopher,' I repeat, 'I feel sorry for you, I really do.'

He takes his hand out again, but only to grope her breasts.

'Did you hear me, Christopher? I feel really sorry for you. I really do.'

Fondling her breast with his left hand, flint against her neck with his right.

'Did you hear me, Christopher?' I repeat, just managing to control my voice.

He stops; turns his head towards me.

'Shut the fuck up. You're next, remember.'

'Really sorry for you,' I repeat.

He looks back down at her.

'I mean, that silly comment you made. The one you thought was so funny, *'mother on daughter action'*, it tells me everything – everything about you. You've never known real love, have you? I mean real love. Sorry for you, Christopher, really, really sorry.'

He turns. I can see I've annoyed him; spoilt his moment.

'Stop fucking well saying that, will you.'

He stands up, his robe falling back over his groin. He walks over to me, stops.

'What we've got, Anna and me, that's love – and you'll never have that. Never. Like I said – sorry for you.'

He towers over me, breathing heavily, red faced, livid – his supreme moment interrupted. 'I thought I told you to shut the fuck up.'

Instantly, he's on me, hands at my throat, round my neck. Strangling the air from me, throttling me.

He's finishing me off. Taking me first. But I'm just looking at him. Straight in the eyes. Not showing fear.

I'm dying, but on my terms. I've screwed up his stupid fucking ceremony. I'll be dead soon – Anna soon after, probably – but who knows, perhaps, somehow, somewhere …

Love must win. Must win.

I start to black out.

From somewhere, a scream. His grip gives. My neck is free.

His hot breath has left me. I open my eyes. His head is being pulled back. Right back, away from me.

'Stop!' screams a voice – a female voice.

It's from behind him, but not Anna, not Su A.

A girl's hand, inches from my face, buries the flint deep into his neck.

A perfect slice – perfect red curve – under left ear, through jugular, under right ear.

Blood. Deep and thick. Gushing over me, over him. Red on white.

He slumps off me.

Lying to my left, his final words: 'Why, Rachel, why …?'

THIRTY-FIVE

AM I ALIVE?

I breathe deeply and open my eyes. Dark ceiling, flickering light.

I can feel the blood. Cold, damp now.

Minutes pass.

My legs. Someone's touching my legs.

I heave myself up, look down.

A torch lights my ankles. The woman's undoing my chains.

I look across the cave. Anna's still there. Breathing. Alive.

Our eyes meet.

'Mum,' she says softly.

'Anna,' I say.

My legs are free. The woman gets up, goes to her. The woman that killed Christopher.

In the other corner, I notice Su A. Cowering. The relationship between Christopher and her was weird. But with this woman? Who is she?

I heave myself up, stumble forward. Past the congealed blood, past the body, to Anna.

I fall to my knees, hug her. Tears in our eyes. I look at her again, we hug again. Seconds, minutes pass.

The woman is still at Anna's feet, sitting. I catch her eyes. Is she – was she – Christopher's partner? The mother of his child?

There's something familiar about her. Familiar, yet perhaps older.

More seconds pass.

'Sorry,' she says. 'I'm sorry.'

I'm honestly not sure why she says that. She's just saved us.

'Do you know the way out?' I ask.

'Yes,' she says.

I help Anna up, wrapping her in one of the blankets. Su A gets up too.

The woman looks down at Christopher's body. A pool of blood, thick and dark, is around his head. Halo of blood.

'Just leave him,' I say. 'That's what the police would want. And don't worry. You'll be OK. You saved us.'

We walk, stumble, down the tunnels – the woman with the torch in front, then Su A, then Anna and me – helping each other.

The cave goes on and on.

She stops. We catch up.

Shining her torch on its entrance, we've reach the denehole. A dark void in the rockface – but this time angling upward. It's not going to be possible for us to go further. Maybe the woman can make it, Su A too, probably. But Anna and I can't.

'Wait here,' says the woman. 'There's a rope – at the top. I'll get it.'

She crouches to go up. Su A is going to follow her.

'Please leave the torch,' I ask.

She pauses, thinks, straightens back up, hands me the torch.

I train the beam on them as they leave. One after the other, they scrabble up the angled opening.

With arm around Anna, I keep the torch on the hole, as dislodged clods of earth fall to the cave floor.

It goes silent again. We wait.

I hear noises. A rope falls through. I go to the hole, bend down, tug at it. It seems firm.

I don't want to leave Anna in this place alone. I let her go first – shining the torch to show her. She hobbles in front.

Slowly, she pulls herself up, earth falling behind her.

Bending down, peering upward, I can see her reach the top. They're helping her, pulling her out.

My turn. Holding the torch in one hand, I grapple my way –
the beam flashing across the faces above me.

Anna's hand. I can just reach Anna's hand. We clasp. The
woman is helping too. Nearly there. They take the torch. One
last effort.

Exhausted, I slump onto the damp earth.

Anna helps me stand up.

We are in the shallow pit. Four of us, in the mudum.

I thank them.

The face of the woman. That's it. Why I recognize her. About
ten years older, maybe. But definitely her. And that's the name
he called her, isn't it?

How do I put it? Do I just say *'It's Rachel, isn't it?'* – like it's
some kind of party? Somehow, it feels wrong. You see, I'm
pretty sure this woman was his partner and I'm also pretty sure
this woman is....

I'll just say her name. It'll sound a little familiar, as if I know
her, but that's all I can do.

'Rachel?'

She looks at me – doesn't say anything.

I think carefully. I'm pretty sure I'm right.

'He was your partner, wasn't he?'

Again, no real response.

I pause. The next question will tell me.

'Your second name, Rachel. What is it?'

Still nothing. I need to put it to her straight. If I look her in the
eye, I'll know.

'It's Baimbridge, isn't it?'

She just looks at me, says nothing. But it's true. It's her.

Rachel Baimbridge.

THIRTY-SIX

A YEAR HAS gone by. The shortest day. I hardly need anniversaries and reminders, though. I think back to that period every day of my life.

You know, I can't say I really blame the police. For not getting there until it was too late, I mean. I didn't exactly crack the case myself, did I? And anyway, when they finally did get there, fighting their way through bracken and bramble, it was still a mighty relief. Anna and I were exhausted and battered, and far from sure that we were fully safe – wary of the brooding Su A.

As for Rachel, she'd gone for help. I wasn't sure I fully trusted her, but had no other option. She was as good as her word, though, contacting the police and leading them back to the edge of the wood. From there, they took over.

McCullough was first to the scene, followed by Wilkins and Pollard – crashing through branches, flashing torches, and shouting out our names. They draped jackets over us, phoned for further assistance and helped us slowly back through the woods – to more bobbies, paramedics and blue flashing lights.

Broken and bruised and with the thud of helicopters overhead, we eventually sped our way to nearby Princess Royal Hospital.

Over the next few weeks, via interviews and statements, everything became a whole lot clearer. You may recall that at one point, when Christopher was in the cave, he said: *'Surprised? Shocked that your little Korean girl doesn't want saving after all?'* It wasn't Su A's acquiescence that was surprising me.

OK, logically she should have welcomed us with open arms. But quite apart from the fact she could barely move them, let alone open them, that's not how it works. We were simply more of the same. She was wary of the police when they turned up, too. She was in a strange land, could hardly speak the language, caged like a dog. How would you feel?

No, it was Christopher's fluent Korean that surprised me. After all, Taplow had insisted that none of his teachers spoke a word of it. As it turned out, the answer was simple. Christopher wasn't a teacher. Just an occasional evening lecturer. I asked for CVs to be checked on teachers, and Edward Taplow, not unreasonably, took it literally. He didn't even have his CV. As it turned out, Christopher had spent ten years in the Far East – Korea, Thailand and the Philippines – doing what, one dare not think.

Various previous cases could probably be attributed to him too, though with his death, they will remain unconfirmed.

Which brings us to Rachel. How had her capture, then compliance come about? Well, Christopher had been a cave guide at the time and, exactly as her mother had belatedly suggested, Rachel had gone there to do some field work on World War II. He'd guided her group and, just as I had done, she asked him some questions towards the end of the tour. Once the other tourists had traipsed away, he'd engaged her in further conversation and then simply dragged her back into the caves, tied her up and kept her there.

But that poses another question. Was he really able to keep her down there undetected for years on end? Simple answer: no. Having softened her up – sensory deprivation is a powerful tool – he eventually took her back to his house in Mottingham. From Rachel's accounts of that period of her life – listless, dreamlike – he probably substituted darkness for drugs. Mind you, he had a small cellar there too. Why, in later years, she didn't make greater efforts to escape is beyond me. You'd need to speak to a psychologist about how that works. Either way, somehow, their relationship stuck, and she went on to bear his child. It was only when she suspected him of extending his abuse to their daughter – by then, aged eight – that she decided to do something about it, digging deeper into his subterranean activities in the process.

As for Su A, Christopher pretty much repeated the formula he'd used during Rachel's early days. Kept her in the cave alive – just – whilst subjecting her to all kinds of abuse. As to what he would eventually have done with her, I couldn't say.

So had he intended to add Anna to this creepy harem too? Almost certainly not. She, like me, was simply to be used for brief pleasure, then sacrificed.

No charges were ever brought against Rachel for the killing of her partner, her sentence – a lifetime of mental anguish – being far worse than anything the state could dish out. On a lesser note, Farrell also walked away without a charge. Given the tiny quantity of drugs recovered, it wasn't worth pursuing. He'll never teach again though.

And what of the long-term damage to us? Well, despite endless counselling and therapy, Anna still suffers from nightmares and seldom goes out alone – even in the daytime. Relationships with boys – Antoine or anyone else – for now, are a no-no. In fact, she may never fully trust a man again. I could joke about that and say it's no bad thing, but it is a serious issue. She will need to get back to a full, rounded life at some stage.

Me? Well, I do think about Edward sometimes – he was certainly very good company on that date. If he rang me up, would I go out with him again? Maybe. But our paths may never cross again. I'm certainly not calling him – ladies of my generation don't do such things. Anyway, as with Anna, all that can wait. We'll get there eventually. We're built of strong stuff, us Andrews girls.

That brings us to the final question. Will we ever get over it – completely, I mean? Probably not. However, I do believe that the first sign of recovery – of something approaching normality – is the return of humour. Not that you can ever look back and laugh, of course. There are certain things way beyond that. But dealing with something, coping with something, is definitely helped by laughing at something. And I can pinpoint that exact moment when laughter, almost, returned.

It happened very recently – about two weeks ago. Anna and I were sitting on the sofa at home. It was getting dark outside, but it wasn't late. We'd already uncorked the wine – after all, there aren't many good things about the shortening days, but uncorking earlier is definitely one of them. I'd made a bit of effort, decorations-wise. My collapsible Christmas tree had been pulled from the cupboard under the stairs, and I'd perched sprigs of holly – taken from the bush in the garden – on picture rails. I can't say I was feeling particularly festive though.

Anna was sitting back, just thinking, and I was halfheartedly flipping through the pages of a magazine.

'Tell you what,' she said, leaning forward and picking her glass up from the table.

'What's that?' I said.

'This year, I'm going to have a Christmas resolution.'

'*Christmas* resolution?' I replied, closing the paper.

'Yes. This year I'm definitely *not* kissing anyone under the mistletoe.'

I got the joke, but her face gave nothing away. Was she being funny or just plain bitter?

There's a silence between us.

Ever so slightly, a nearly-smile creeps onto her face. Then it slowly broadens. I smile too.

We embrace. We laugh … well, almost.

'Yes,' I say. 'This year, absolutely *no* kissing under the mistletoe.'